Bradon: Encouraged to Overcome

The Barnabas Chronicles
Book 4

By

Ronna M. Bacon

Deuteronomy 31:6 Be strong and of a good courage, fear not, nor be afraid of them: for the LORD your God, he it is that does go with you; he will not fail you, nor forsake you.

Psalm 9:9-10 The LORD also will be a refuge for the oppressed, a refuge in times of trouble. And they that know your name will put their trust in you: for you, LORD, have not forsaken them that seek you.

Table of Contents

With a light breeze blowing in his face, Bradon Cahill stood on the edge of a cliff, his deep blue eyes focused on Lake Erie, watching the roll of the waves crashing against the rocks. He drew in a deep breath, needing, he thought, to clear his lungs. He had been away from his home for the last couple of days, evaluating dogs for a security company. He missed his red merle Australian Shepherd, Kade, but had decided he needed to take a break on the way home. That's why he stood, overlooking the lake, feeling lonely for some reason. Lord, I know You are with me, but seeing Baird, Benen, and Blair all finding their ladies, I wish I had my own lady. But You know best. Help me to be content.

Turning, Bradon walked away from the cliff, shifting his pack to a more comfortable position, his eyes searching the area, not seeing anything wrong, but with a niggling feeling in the back of his neck, he knew something was about to happen, and he had no idea what.

He felt the wind picking up and turned to look back at the lake, seeing the dark clouds moving in from the other side. He shivered, knowing that rain would likely happen and he wasn't near his truck, not close enough if the rain happened soon.

Bradon paused, a frown on his face as he heard voices, one raised in anger. His head tilting, he listened and then began to run. That's a female voice and I can hear fear in it, he thought. Lord, protect her. I'm not sure I can get there fast enough.

He paused at a clearing, seeing a young person, he thought, struggling to escape from the hands that held her wrists tight. Without thinking, he was racing through the grass, launching himself at the man, and taking him to the ground. The three hit hard, before Bradon's fist met the man's chin and then he was on his feet, his hand reaching to pull the young person up and with him as he ran back the way he had come, his head turning to watch the man.

Turning back to pull on the hand he had tight in his, he caught a glimpse of dark brown eyes and blond hair. She's beautiful and my age, was his thought before she tugged at his hand, taking him down another path.

She finally slid to a halt, her hand to her throat, as she peered behind him, waving her other hand at him to keep quiet. She leaned against a tree, her breath coming in gasps, as she turned her attention to him.

"Thank you, I think."

"What do you mean, you think?" Bradon was astounded at her words. "Were you not just being assaulted?" His hand ran through his red-gold hair, ruffling the curls he tried to keep short.

"I guess. I'm sorry. I didn't mean it the way it sounded." She looked back up the path and down towards the end of it. "This will lead us out to the lake and then we can work our way around."

"I'm sorry? What did you just say?"

"I said we can go down there and get away." Her finger stabbed in the air as she pointed.

"That's what I thought you said." He looked around. "What was his problem?"

She shook her head. "You don't want to know." She studied him for a moment. "You're not from here."

"No, I'm not. I'm Bradon Cahill."

"I'm Ennis Dacre." She moved away, her head tilted to look up. "We need to move. There's a storm moving in and the area we need to cross floods with the lake tide."

Bradon shook his head as he followed her. "I still want to know what that man wanted."

Ennis spun, her mouth open to speak as the wind suddenly picked up. Bradon gave a yell, throwing himself at her, taking them to the ground, tucking Ennis under him as he heard a crack and saw the shadow of a fir tree heading their way. His arms covered their heads even as Ennis shoved at him, to get him to move. Bradon felt the thud of a branch against him and lost the battle to keep his eyes open.

He roused later, how much later he wasn't sure, and pushed at the ground, a groan escaping him at the pain in his shoulder. He squinted against the pain, before his eyes dropped to Ennis, finding her unconscious. Lord, what happened? Who was that she was fighting with?

His head dropped back as he heard low angry voices near him, one he was sure belonging to the man who had assaulted Ennis. What was that all about? His eyes closed as he lost the battle to stay focused and awake. He needed to get them out of there but couldn't.

Ennis stirred later, sometime after Bradon had dropped back into the well of blackness. She heard voices and twisted her body, trying to shove Bradon away from her and not succeeding. Her voice filled with pain, she answered the calls for her, bringing her brother and father towards the tree.

"Ennis? Are you under there?" Her brother, Evan, crouched down, carefully working through the smaller branches until he found her. "And who's this?"

"His name is Bradon. He saved me. We need to get him out of here."

"And we will. Here, can you move? Let me have your hand."

Reaching for her brother's hand, Ennis carefully crawled towards him, feeling Bradon's body falling to the ground behind her. She was out from under the tree and in her father's arms, before she spun, crouching down to watch as Evan carefully maneuvered Bradon from under the fir.

"Where's he hurt, son?" Ian Dacre's voice was quiet, his eyes studying the younger man.

"A shoulder, I think, Dad. He's got some blood on his head as well." Evan stared down at him and then up at his father. "I don't like to move him."

"We don't have much choice. There's more wind and rain moving in. Here, let's get him up and over your shoulders. Ennis, stand back. You're not hurt, lass?"

"I don't think so. I knocked myself out when I went down, I think. Likely, I'll have some bruises. But we need to get him out of here. Jason was around again, and Bradon saved me from him."

Ian and Evan exchanged a glance before Bradon was over Evan's shoulders and the four were moving out. Ian stood for a moment as they neared the beach, his eyes looking backwards. His heart was heavy for his daughter, knowing that the man who had haunted her steps for so many years was back. How do we keep her safe, Lord? We can't restrict her movements. His eyes turned ahead to study his son, and then Bradon. Is he the one, Lord? Is he the one who will help her overcome what has happened in the past? If so, thank you. If not, guard both their hearts.

Ennis' hand came out to touch Bradon's face as Evan paused for a moment at the foot of the path.

"Go ahead, Ennis. The truck just up ahead. You'll need to sit in the back with him." Evan watched her closely, a frown on his face, before he moved forward.

None of them saw the two men standing up on the cliff, watching intently as they moved away. Nor could they hear the angry words exchanged between the two before the man called Jason followed along the cliff, just long enough to see Ennis disappear into her brother's truck.

Chapter 2

Ian had dug Bradon's keys out of his jacket pocket and then followed Evan home with his truck. He shook his head. Now, what? Who is this young man and where is he from? Questions raced through his mind, knowing they would have to wait until Bradon regained consciousness.

Evan gently dropped Bradon onto the antique maple wooden bed in the main floor guest room, and then stood back, breathing heavily for a moment, before his hands reached to remove Bradon's boots and set them neatly to one side. His father had reached for Bradon's pack and dropped it to the arm chair before he eased the jacket from him and then his shirt.

"How bad is it, Dad?" Evan watched carefully as Ennis stood by the bed, her arms wrapped around herself. "Ennis. You need to get cleaned up and into dry clothes. Go. We'll call you back when we're ready." Evan's hands were gentle on his sister as he moved her from the room, a frown on his face at the look in her eyes before his head turned to watch Bradon.

Ennis stood for a moment before she ran for the room she was using at the moment in her parents' home. She had just moved back home, accepting work in a town nearby as a medical office assistant. She wasn't too sure about this, wanting her independence but knowing she needed time to accept the fact that she was back in her home area and knowing she needed to decide just where she would live. She twisted her long hair into a clip as the final step to dry, clean clothes and gathered her wet things, throwing them into the washer on the way by back on the first floor, to head for the kitchen and something hot. Ennis' hand rested on the kettle as her headed turned towards the hallway before she sighed. No, she thought. He can't be the knight on the white charger coming to my rescue, now can he? Even though his truck is white? Lord, why do I trust him to quickly? It's not me to trust like that.

Her mother, Meg, stood for a moment, her eyes on her daughter before she swept her into a hug.

"This is not how we wanted you to come home."

"I know, Mom. I thought I was safe out there today. I was so careful. Made sure no one followed me." Ennis blinked back tears, tears she vowed would not fall. She had shed enough tears over that man, now hadn't she, Lord?

"But who is this man that your Dad and brother are working on? Your Dad just said they found you two under a fallen fir tree." Meg drew her daughter down to a chair, placing their tea cups on the table and then reaching for a plate of homemade scones.

"I don't know, Mom. Jason had me by the wrist and I was trying to get away. In Mel's clearing. Next thing I know, I'm on the ground and Bradon has knocked Jason out. He grabbed hold of me and we ran. We were heading for Mel's beach when the wind picked up and brought down the tree." She paused. "Who is he, Mom? And where did he come from? There wasn't anyone else around, not that I saw."

Meg looked up as Ian paused in the doorway. "When he's awake, we'll ask him. Ian?"

Ennis raised her head as her father sat beside her, reaching to give her a hug.

"I am so glad he was there, Ennis. I don't want to think of what might have happened."

"Has he been awake?"

Ian shrugged. "Just briefly to ask if you were safe."

"How is he, Dad? Do we need to take him to the hospital?" Ennis rubbed her hands on her mug, her eyes on it, as she waited for her father to speak.

"No, I don't think so. Evan has had a good look at him. His shoulder is bruised and he won't be using that arm for a while. The head has a bump on it, but not as bad as we had thought. We'll wait and take him in when he awakens. The rain is starting to pick up again as is the wind."

She nodded before she rose and walked away, leaving her parents to stare after her before they exchanged glances and then bowed their heads to pray for their girl and for the stranger they found in their home. Somehow, they both knew his coming would make a difference for her.

Ennis stood for a moment in the bedroom doorway before she approached the bed and sank into the chair her father had pulled close to it. She studied the man lying there, a frown on her face. She thought she knew him but that was impossible. She shook her head. There was no way she had met him before. Ennis didn't think she would have forgotten him. Her head bowed as she too prayed for him.

Bradon's eyes flickered open and he frowned as he glanced around. This wasn't his bedroom. That much he knew. But where was he? His eyes stopped as they landed on Ennis, and his face softened. She's here, he thought. She's here and she's safe. Pulling his hand from beneath the blanket, he grimaced with the pain from his other shoulder. This is not good, he thought.

Ennis jumped as she felt a hand touch her, and her head raised rapidly, her eyes huge as she stared at the hand on hers and then at Bradon.

"You're awake?"

"I am. It's Ennis? I'm saying it right?"

"You are. How are you feeling?"

"Sore. What did I do to shoulder?" He moved to raise himself up, a groan coming from him as he do, Ennis reaching to tuck pillows behind him.

"Evan thinks it's just bruised. He's a physiotherapist, in case you need one."

Bradon shot her a quick look, catching the sparkle of mischief in the brown eyes that he felt he could get lost in. "He is? Is he taking me to the hospital to verify that?"

"The weather's too bad. It's gotten really windy and the rain is quite heavy. There are severe thunderstorm and a tornado warning out."

"Is that what hit the tree?"

She shook her head, her braid swaying with the movement. "No, just a heavy wind. That tree's been ready to fall for years."

"And it had to wait until we were under it, did it?" His head went back for a moment as his eyes closed. "Any chance for a shower? And are my clothes dry?"

"I'll get Evan to help you, if you need to. He's brought in your pack. Are there clothcs in it?"

Bradon shook his head. "Is my truck here?"

"Dad brought it back for you. By the way, you're at my parents' place for now." She studied him, her head tilting to the side in a movement that fascinated him. "Do you have luggage in it?"

"There's a duffle bag in the back seat. It has some clean clothes." He groaned again and looked around.

"What do you need?" Ennis watched him closely.

"My phone. Did you see it?"

"We did. It's charging right now. Mom plugged it in out in the kitchen." She watched him closely for a moment and then walked away, Bradon watching her every move, something about her drawing him to her.

Now what, Lord? What did I do when I went to help her? And how do I keep her safe? He didn't see Evan watching him, his own heart praying for his sister, with a wish that just maybe someone had come into her life.

Evan watched later as Bradon sat in the kitchen, a quiet word of thanks to Meg for the cup of coffee and plate of toast that she slid in front of him, before his eyes raised to his sister, who was standing just out of Bradon's sight, her own eyes on the stranger in their house. He caught the wishful look of longing on her face and his heart broke for his sister, knowing that she had so much to give and had been chased from her own home for years, just to try and stay safe. Evan felt the anger beginning to grow in him and then felt his father's hand on his shoulder.

Chapter 3

A few hours later, sitting in the living room, Ennis watched Bradon once more as he spoke with her parents, Evan beside her, a frown on his face. He felt he knew Bradon from somewhere but wasn't quite sure.

"Where do you work, Bradon?" Ian was curious, his eyes narrowing as he caught a glimpse of Ennis' face, and decided they needed to learn more about the young man.

"I work for K9 specialties. We evaluate and also train dogs for security companies and also for individuals that need one." Bradon looked down for a moment, biting at his lip, before he looked up, deciding he could trust this family with something that was not common knowledge. "I am actually employed by The Barnabas Foundation, which pays my wages. I work for K9S."

"The Barnabas Foundation? Barnabas Carey?" At Bradon's nod, Ian continued. "I know his father quite well. We've attended many men's conferences at the same time." He studied Bradon closer. "I heard some of your friends have had their adventures."

Bradon grinned, the smile lighting up his face. "That they have. First it was Baird and Berneen. Then Benen and Cadee. Blair and his Devaney just survived theirs a few months ago."

Ennis gave a soft laugh. "Three of your friends? What kind of adventures would they have?"

Bradon kept grinning, even as he shook his head. "No one believes us." He sobered. "It was so dangerous for them, and for those of us who got caught in it. Baird had been kidnapped, taken to where Berneen was being held. Some of us went in and rescued them, only to have them kidnapped again with our friend and pastor, Buckley. To save his life, Berneen agreed to marry him. They are such a wonderful couple. They faced some pretty tough and hard difficulties.

"Then, there's Benen and Cadee, friends for years. Her parents were missionaries. Long story short - there was a contract out on Cadee and the only way to get her out safely was a name change. Benen agreed to marry her, brought her back from the country the mission was in. Similar dangers to the first couple.

"And then there was Blair and Devaney. They were in the same foster home, fell in love, decided to marry, and then Devaney walked away because someone threatened Blair's life. She made her way across the country from Alberta, ending up here and reuniting with Blair."

"There is no way that happened!" Ennis snapped her mouth shut. "It can't. It doesn't happen in real life."

Bradon began to laugh, causing the others to stare at him. "I'm sorry. Each of the ladies have said the same thing. It can only happen on television or in books or movies."

Evan began to grin. "And how many of you are there?"

"With Barnabas, there are fourteen of us who live in the Foundation Building. Ian, I think you've likely seen it?"

Ian nodded. "I have. It's been years, but if I recall, it was set up to provide housing for all of you, as well as Doc and Anna?"

"Doc and Anna Adams are still there. She mothers us all. He's the father none of us can remember or haven't had for years." He sobered, realizing just how true that was for himself. His parents had been killed in a home invasion when he was young and staying at a friend's overnight. He had lived with his maternal grandparents until they both died just as he became an adult.

"I know Doc." Evan spoke up. "I can see him fulfilling that role." He paused, his eyes on Ennis. "Now what, Bradon? You're not able to drive and I know you're anxious to get home."

Bradon nodded, his eyes catching a movement from Ennis that stopped his eyes on her face, a frown flitting across his.

"No, I can't drive, not a standard transmission. I mean I could, but is someone volunteering?"

"Ennis will." Evan just grinned at his sister as she spun on the couch, her mouth dropping open before she snapped it shut and then glared at him. "She can drive standard. In fact, she's the best of all of us at that."

"If you don't want to, Ennis, that's fine. I'll just one of the guys a call and they'll come get me. Or I can attempt the drive. I'm sure I can manage it."

She shook her head. "No, it's fine. Evan can follow us or I'll just load my bike on your truck."

Bradon stared at her. "Your bike? After what happened earlier today?"

Ennis nodded. "I don't let him control my life. If I want to bike, I will." She was on her feet, moving from the room, and they heard the back door shut quietly behind her.

Bradon's head went back. "What did I say I shouldn't have?"

"It's not what you said, Bradon." Meg spoke up, her eyes on Evan and his reaction to his sister's departure. "It's that she doesn't want to give him any more control over her life than he has had. She's lived away from here since she was twenty. That's eight years or so we missed out on the day to day interaction with her because of him. She has come home. Ennis is determined to stop him somehow and that makes us afraid for her. She will not let him win this time and drive her away."

Bradon had been watching Meg closely. "And she needs someone to step in? Someone not her family?"

Ian nodded. "That's exactly what she needs and what she refuses to ask for. We can only do so much. She is an adult and even though we worry about her, we have to let her live her life." He paused. "She's moving to your town, Bradon. I know it's only twenty miles from here but he will track her down."

Shaking his head, his eyes on Evan, Bradon hesitated to ask. "What is the issue? I don't want to misstep if I say something to her."

"We have all done that at some point, Bradon." Meg's hand rubbed about the arm of the chair she was seated in. "He had fixated on her, demanding that she date only him, intending her to be his possession is how she has phrased it. She has not told us everything that he has said, but I know it can't be pretty. She's been badly hurt by him and that has coloured her relationships with others and how she views herself at times. Her faith is strong, but sometimes that just isn't enough in a young woman's life."

He shook his head. "That shouldn't happen." He was on his feet, heading for the back door, searching for his shoes to slip them on, finding his jacket hanging up on the coat rack. He slipped into it, his hand reaching for the door before he pulled it open and stood outside, the door closing behind him.

Ennis stood, her arm wrapped around a porch column. He could see the dejection and fear in her stance. Bradon moved to stand near her, not saying anything.

"Bradon?"

"It shouldn't have happened, Ennis. He shouldn't have been allowed to treat you the way he has."

She shrugged. "No one has been able to get through to him. And what you did? You've made yourself an enemy. He's brutal."

"Who all has he threatened?"

Ennis spun, her mouth dropping open. "What do you mean?"

"He has threatened someone close to you. Your parents? Evan?" He watched her closely. "He's threatened to physically harm you or worse, hasn't he?"

She nodded, tears clouding her eyes for a moment. "Thank you."

"Thank you? For what?" Bradon's voice softened, even as he heard the sound of the rain thumping on the metal roof overhead and felt the faint spray hitting him when the wind blew it towards him.

"You're the first one who has verbalized that. I couldn't say anything. Evan would have been after him."

Bradon just reached for her. "Come here, sweetheart." He gathered her close, her arms around him, hugging him tight. He could feel the shudders running through her. "I won't let him hurt you. Not ever. Not I can help it."

"But how?" Her voice was hopeful, muffled as it was with her head buried against him.

"I'll stop him and I have thirteen friends who will help."

Ennis stared at him, her mouth dropping open at his words. He gave her a gentle smile as he tapped her chin, causing her to close her mouth.

"I have thirteen friends, one of the Barnabas Carey. The other twelve are employed by the Foundation. I also have a multitude of others I can call in. You will be safe."

She shook her head. "No, I won't. I haven't been in years."

He gave her a gentle smile. "You will be. I've found my lady, God willing, and I won't let anything happen to her." He dropped a kiss on her forehead and then, turning, walked back into the house, leaving her staring after him, a hand covering her mouth, tears sparkling on her cheeks she didn't know she was shedding.

Is he the one, Lord? Is he the knight I've dreamed about and begged You for?

Chapter 4

The next afternoon, Branigan Clery and Benen Carroll, two of Bradon's friends, sat in one of the garden areas, idle conversation between them, Bradon's dog, Kade, stretched out at their feet. They had fully expected Bradon back yesterday and were becoming concerned because no one had heard from him, unusual for their group of friends.

Kade's head raised as they heard a vehicle coming to a stop, and then, with a low bark, he was away, knowing he had heard Bradon's truck. The two men shrugged and then rose, following him, anxious to know that Bradon was fine.

Their steps slowed as the driver's door opened, Kade stopping and then approaching the person who dropped down to the ground.

"That's not Bradon, but it's his truck." Branigan walked forward as the passenger door opened and Bradon stepped down, his hand out to greet Kade, whose whole body was wriggling with excitement that his master was home, before he walked around to where Ennis stood, uncertainty in her stance, his free hand going out for hers.

"Are you sure this is okay?" She was hesitant as he turned her towards the building.

"I'm sure." His steps stopped as he saw his two friends. "Ennis, I want you to meet Branigan and Benen."

She gave a small smile, her hand tightening on his, as he made the introductions.

"Bradon? What did you go and do? Can't let you out of our sight, is that it?" Branigan's voice broke through the short silence that ensued Bradon's introduction.

"I saved a lady in distress and then tangled with a fir tree. It's just bruised. I'll have Doc check it out." He shook his head slightly at them. "Is Barnabas around?"

"He will be later. We were wondering where you were. Kade was getting quite anxious."

Bradon laughed as he looked down at his dog, who by this time had plastered himself to Ennis' side, his eyes watchful, knowing somehow she was in danger. He nodded.

"I need to talk to him. Ennis here needs our help, and a place to stay that's safe."

"Another lady in distress?" Benen grinned. "I need to introduce you to Cadee."

"Cadee? She's the one from South America?" Ennis frowned as she tried to remember what Bradon had said.

"She was when I married her, but she's originally from my home town." Benen pointed towards the door. "How be we go in? I know she's around."

Ennis didn't move, her eyes now glued to Kade. Bradon could feel the shudders running through her and ducked his head to watch her face, seeing the fear, no terror, he thought, on her face before his eyes moved to Kade. A quiet word had Kade moving backwards and sitting, his eyes still on Ennis.

"Ennis?" Bradon's voice was quiet, a frown on his face, even as his two friends watched the pair closely. He didn't see Baird and Brady approaching, nor others of his friends gathering around, the three young ladies walking towards him. "Ennis? What is it?"

"Your dog."

"Yes, Kade's my dog. What about it?"

"I can't be near dogs. I'm sorry." She turned, her body ready to run, before his arm wrapped around her. "I'm sorry."

"What are you sorry about?" His eyes lifted to his friends, seeing their concern before they slid shut. "What did he do?"

"His dog. It attacked me. I can't do dogs." Her voice was thick with her tears. "I'm sorry. He looks like a nice dog."

"He is. He is very gentle. And he is worried about you. That's why he was so close to you. He won't attack." A small grin appeared on Bradon's face. "He'll protect you."

Branigan spoke up. "Bradon's right. Kade will protect you. He has seen you two together. He sees Bradon holding your hand. In Kade's mind, that makes you important to Bradon. That makes you his family, and he will protect his family. He did that to protect one of our ladies."

Ennis' eyes raised to his for a moment before they dropped back to Kade. "I'm sorry."

—

27

"Ennis?"   Bradon's quiet question had her looking at him. "Where did you get bit? And what kind of dog?"

"A mastiff mix, I think. I'm not sure now. I've tried too hard to forget it. I wouldn't go with him and he set the dog on me." Her face whitened even more at the memory.

"How many stitches? And where?"

"My right calf. About thirty or more, I think. I didn't want to know." Ennis' head turned back into Bradon's shoulder, not seeing the shock on his face or on the faces of those listening.

Bradon shook his head at his friends, turning Ennis to walk into the building, seeing Breck, the second in command at the Foundation, walking his way. A quick word and Bradon was leading Ennis into the building and to a suite near his. He knew someone would grab his duffle bag and backpack. He didn't have to ask.

Ennis finally looked up and around the suite, her mouth opening and closing at the comfortable look of the apartment. She walked slowly through, before she returned, to stand in front of Bradon, a question on her face.

"You can stay here, Ennis. Breck has okayed it."

"He did? I didn't meet him, did I?"

Bradon grinned as he shook his head. "Not yet, but he was out there. Now, about this guy?"

She nodded. "I need to talk to someone. I'm just not sure who. We have put in complaints. We tried to have him charged with his dog attacked me. All for nothing. The police officer wouldn't even take a statement from us. I have it all documents. Medical records. What have you. It's all in writing. No one in my family knows the extent of what I have been through."

"They know, sweetheart. They have a pretty good idea. Your father hasn't acted, not yet, but he will if this continues."

Chapter 5

Looking for Bradon later that afternoon, Barnabas' feet slowed as he found Ennis in one of the gardens, Kade near her, but no Bradon. He had talked to Breck and then to Branigan, who had brought him up to date as much as they could. There were gaps they didn't know the answers to, and that he needed to speak with either Bradon or Ennis.

Ennis spun as she heard steps behind her, backing up and away from Barnabas, who paused in his forward walk to study her, Kade rising and coming to stand in front of her, eyes on Barnabas.

"I'm sorry. I didn't mean to frighten you." A grin broke through the grimness on Barnabas' face. "I'm Barnabas Carey."

"Dad knows you."

"Your father?"

"At least I think he does. He knows your father. My dad is Ian Dacre."

Barnabas nodded, the grin staying on his face. "He does indeed. Dad has mentioned him many times. But that doesn't explain why you are here."

Ennis shook her head. "I knew this was a bad idea. I'll leave as soon as I can get someone to take me home." She didn't see Bradon approaching her or the look on his face that said he didn't want her to do that.

"No, it's fine. Dad would want you to stay here. So do I. I understand you will be working in our town. This makes sense to have you here."

"But it doesn't mean I'll be safe, does it?" She brushed by him, hesitating as she saw Bradon, and then almost running for the building.

"Barnabas?" Bradon's voice had his friend turning.

"You're okay?"

Bradon shrugged, pain flickering across his face for a moment. "I talked to Doc. It's bruised from what he can tell. About Ennis?"

"Yes. About Ennis. Talk to me, Bradon. I know there's more than what you have said."

"There is." Bradon turned to walk back towards the building, anxious to find Ennis. He described what he had happened upon and what had happened to him, then went on to tell him what Ennis had confirmed about Jason.

"They did nothing?" Barnabas had to tamp down anger. "I'll talk to her parents, see what they can tell us."

Bradon shook his head. "I should be the one. Right now, she's not sure who she can trust. She's lived away for so long." He paused, his hand rubbing at his injured shoulder. "Breck said she could have the one suite."

"She can, for as long as she needs to. I understand from him that she's working here?"

"She is. I know she'll want her independence. And I can't say I fault her for that, but if needed, she can always catch a ride with one of us." He looked down at the sling. "And I have to talk to Rick."

"Yes, you do. But I know him. You'll be able to continue working, even in a sling." Barnabas gave a small wave as he moved away.

Ennis had stood just inside the building door, not seeing the lobby or the seating areas Barnabas had set up. The security guard on duty stood watching her, knowing that she was Bradon's lady in everyone's mind and that she was in trouble. She watched as Bradon walked her way, not seeing Kade standing as close to her as he could get.

"Bradon? Can you take me home?" Her heartbroken voice stopped him in his tracks.

He stared at her, then with a hand on her arm, directed her to a seating area, waiting for her to sit before he sat beside her.

"Why?" His voice was quiet.

"Why? Because I need to. I can't stay here."

"And why can't you?"

"Because I can't. It puts you at risk."

"Actually, we've been there and done that." He grinned at her and held up three fingers. "Each of the ladies brought trouble here. We didn't let that stop us helping them, and it won't stop us helping you. Barnabas has said you are to use the suite I showed you to. That's a given. And if you're not comfortable driving back and forth, then one of us will take you. We all work in town. When we're not working, we volunteer."

"You volunteer?" Her mind refused to take in that she had been offered a sanctuary. "What do you volunteer at?"

"The community garden. I find it a nice change of pace." He grinned at the look on her face. 'Didn't see that coming, I guess?"

Ennis shook her head, leaning back on the couch, her hand rubbing at the leather. "These are nice." She looked up, surprise on her face, at the second seating area. "This is quite the building."

"It is. Barnabas and his father spent a lot of time designing it. They're expanding the facilities outside now."

"They are?" Ennis grew quiet, not quite sure where she stood with Bradon or even his friends. "Bradon? If I'm to stay, I need my things."

"Your parents thought of that. All you have to do is call them. They will gladly bring your things, as you call it, but they are sad that it has to come to this."

"I know. He's taken so much." Her eyes slid closed. "I don't think he's working on his own. That's the thing. Someone is working with him." She looked up at Bradon. "And I don't know why he's fixated on me. It doesn't make sense. I had no contact with him before it all started."

"And how old were you?" Bradon's arm swept her into a hug. "How old, sweetheart?"

"I never told anyone when it first started. I thought it would go away. I was like sixteen, almost seventeen."

Bradon's eyes slid closed. So young, he thought, and to have had to carry that all these years, leaving home to protect her family and now that she's back, it will start up again.

Chapter 6

Ennis turned from the kitchen in her suite, a smile on her face as she listened to her father teasing her brother. I can do this, she thought, before she looked over at her mother, who stood, fridge door open, putting away the groceries they had brought for her.

"You didn't have to do that, Mom?"

Meg looked up, a smile on her face. "But we did. You know your father. He had to shop for you, to make sure you had enough to eat. Although, I do think he shopped for himself as well."

Ennis started to laugh, causing her mother to join in. "I'm sure he did. He can't hover, though, Mom. I can't have that."

"We know, dear, but you are his little girl. Always will be. Even when you marry, you'll still be that."

Ennis gave a snort, causing her mother to break out into fresh laughter. "I don't see that happening, Mom."

Meg just shook her head, her eyes on Bradon as he stood watching from the kitchen doorway, his heart in his eyes. Ennis wasn't ready for that, not just yet, she thought. Lord, protect these two. They are walking into something, and need that protection. Protect their hearts, please, dear Lord, and if she's the one for him and he for her, work it out for them.

Bradon moved towards the two ladies, his hands out to take the boxes from Ennis. "I'll get rid of these for you, unless you want to keep them?" Her head shook at his question. "All settled?"

"I think so." She looked around. "Where's your dog?"

Her question had her parents spinning and staring at her, knowing how she was so fearful of dogs.

"I left him in my suite. He's fine."

"No, it's not. He hasn't seen you in days. And I know he goes with you wherever you go here." She looked up, distressed. "I can't have you putting him away. I knew this was not such a good idea."

Her father's arm around her shoulder stopped her words. "I'm sure Bradon is comfortable with that. If he's not, he'll talk to you." Ian paused, not quite sure how to phrase his next sentence. "It has always distressed us that Jason took your love of dogs away. Maybe Bradon's dog will bring that back. I've met him. He's a beautiful dog, gentle in nature."

"That he is, Ian. And now that he's seen Ennis with me, he'll protect her."

Ennis was shaking her head. "He can't do that."

"But he will. It's in his nature to protect my friends." Bradon's hand gently touched her cheek. "Now, how be we head into town? You can show me where you work, and your parents and Evan can join us for a meal?"

"We can do that, I think." Ennis turned to her family, finding them nodding. "Well, okay, then."

Bradon watched her later as he drove back to the building. She had relaxed some but he could see she was still uncertain as to the wisdom of her move. She would relax, he prayed, knowing that once Berneen, Cadee, and Devaney spoke with her, she would find friends who would understand what she was going through. He knew it was tough on her parents to walk away, even though they lived close. Evan had made a point to speak with him, asking that Bradon keep him updated as to what was going on, and he would do the same. He had a friend, a private investigator, he would be speaking with, he stated. It didn't matter that Ennis had told him not to in the past. This time, they needed it over for her, he said.

Ennis' head turned as she watched the sky. "It's such a beautiful night."

"It is." Bradon's face held contentment for the moment. "We have a beach on the property. I'll show you tomorrow."

"Do you have bike trails?"

"Bike trails?" Bradon shot her a quick glance.

"Yes, bike trails. You know. Those trails you ride your bike on. I love to bike, and Dad brought mine."

"He did? We do, but I would just ask that you let one of us know when you're heading out. Even if it's just the security guard."

"About that. Why have a security guard?"

"Just for protection. The Barnabas Foundation is worth billions." He grinned as her mouth dropped open. "Barnabas' father insisted we have security. Although the culprits can still get to our ladies when they want to."

"They can? So, this security? It's that good?"

Bradon had pulled into his parking spot by that time and at her words, shot her a look, his eyes narrowing at the gleam of mischief in hers. "It's not their fault. They do their best. It's when the ladies are out and about that they seem to run into difficulty. And that makes it hard for us guys to take care of our ladies."

"About that. You keep calling me that. And you have your friends doing the same."

"I do? I guess they've picked up on something." Bradon stared out the windshield, his hand rubbing at his arm. Driving had put a stress on it, but he hadn't let Ennis drive that afternoon. "I think of you as that, Ennis. I know you're not ready, may never be ready for that." He slipped from the truck, coming around to open her door, reaching for her hand to help her down and then not letting go.

"We do need to talk. But right now, you need to rest your arm. You haven't and I can see the pain in your face."

Chapter 7

Spotting the white envelope under her windshield wiper, Ennis hesitated to approach her car after her work had ended for the day. He's found me, hasn't he, Lord? And too soon. How do I stay safe and keep everyone around me safe? She hesitated to touch it but finally reached to pull it out, her key fob out to unlock her car door. She was inside and the doors locked in just a few seconds.

Ennis stared at the envelope before dropping it onto the seat beside her. She didn't need to read it to know what he would say. She had brought danger to Bradon. And in doing so, she had brought danger to his friends.

Bradon was waiting for her, a frown on his face as he saw the disheartened look on hers.

"Ennis? What did he do?" He glanced at the envelope in her hand. "Where did you find it?"

"Under the wiper blade." She looked up at him, a shuttered look on her face. "I can't do this anymore, Bradon. I just can't."

His hand reaching for the envelope, he then swung his arm around her, directing her to the building. "We'll open this and then pass it on to whoever it needs to go to. I had a chance to talk to our police chief today. He's concerned. He'll want to talk to you at some point."

"What is the point of that? Nothing will get done."

"On the contrary, there will be."

A voice behind her had a small scream coming from her as she jumped and spun. Will Peters stood there, waiting for Bradon to introduce them.

"Ennis, this is our police chief and good friend, Will Peters." Bradon made the introductions, then handed Will the envelope. "She found this just a bit ago, Will. We haven't opened it."

Will nodded, his eyes on the envelope before he looked up. "Can we head for your office, Bradon? Ennis? Do you need to change or anything before we talk?"

She finally nodded. "If I could. I always change when I come home. Where's your office, Bradon?"

He grinned. "I'll wait here for you."

Ennis stared at him for a moment before she was off, almost on a run. Will and Bradon watched her go before Will spoke.

"I talked to her father today after we spoke. He called me. When he told me the name of the officer, I can see why it didn't go anywhere. It's not common knowledge, but he is connected to this man."

"And he was let investigate?"

Will nodded. "I have spoken with the chief there. He wasn't aware of the connection at the time or it would never have happened. That officer has been dismissed from the force. He had too many complaints such as hers to let him stay on."

Bradon sighed. "And if he hadn't been the one, this could have never gotten to this point."

"We don't know that. From what I understand, it likely would have. I have asked Dallas to take a look at what we have and decide from there where we go."

"Dallas. That's good. We'll need to connect with him at some point." Bradon reached for Ennis' hand as she stopped once more beside him. "Kade's in my office. Is that okay?"

She shrugged. "I guess. Just don't let him near me."

Will frowned. "There's a problem with Kade?"

"Not with Kade, per se. But with dogs. This monster let his dog attack her years ago, and she ended up with multiple stitches."

Will shook his head. "We'll stop him, Ennis."

"Before or after he kills someone? He's quite capable of that."

Will sank into a chair in Bradon's office, his eyes on Kade for a moment as he rubbed the dog's head. "I get that, Ennis. That's what we want to avoid."

"And can we do that?"

"We will do our best to prevent that. You're an important part of our family now, Ennis." Will watched Bradon as he spoke, the younger man's head nodding at the words. "Now, about this envelope?"

———

41

"Yes, that. Please? Just make him go away. You have no idea how much I have prayed for just that."

"I have a good idea on that, Ennis. Before I open this, what all has he done? How many times have you had something like this?"

Ennis shrugged. "About two dozen I would say. None when I was living away from home, but I would find evidence I was being watched. Footprints in the garden around the house. The odd photo that showed up. He was really bad before I left."

"And just what did he do?" Will had his notebook and pen out, taking notes.

"He threatened to hurt me. He threatened to hurt my family, even threatening to kill them. But nothing that said why he was. And I found that strange. He would approach me at times, trying to make me go with him. His dog, he set him on me once." She shook with fear at that memory, not realizing that Kade had approached her and laid his chin on her knee, his eyes on her face. Her hand laid on his head without her knowing she had done that, finding comfort in touching him.

"That dog attack? It was reported?"

Ennis nodded. "We did but he had hidden the dog, said it was a stray that attacked me. It was his word against mine. I ended up with the stitches, a scar, and having to take rabies shots."

"That shouldn't have happened. I have spoken with the police chief in your town. The responding officer is not on the force anymore. The chief sends his apologies, although that cannot change the fact that this was mishandled and mishandled badly."

"It's what I expected. I figured that officer was a friend of Jason's." She sank back in her chair, her eyes focusing on Kade as he sat near her, his chin still on her knee. "Bradon? Your dog?"

Bradon grinned at her. "He does that when he thinks someone is upset. It's his way of comforting that person. You're not the first lady he's approached like that."

She nodded, her fear of dogs starting to rise within her, before she sighed and then prayed for that to be over as well.

"What's in the envelope, Will?" Bradon's question had Will fingering the envelope.

Will pulled latex gloves onto his hands before he opened the envelope. A single photo dropped out. "When did you two go to the restaurant?"

"Last Saturday. We were with my parents and brother. Why?"

He held up the photo. "This is taken there, as you are leaving. He's following you, Ennis."

"Of course he is. Isn't that what they always do?"

Chapter 8

Will had spoken to the young couple for close to an hour, Ennis being as honest as she could with everything. He had frowned as he heard how young she had been when it started, and that no one had stepped up to stop it for her. He would need to speak with Dallas. He wanted this stopped before it went any further, but he knew that would not happen.

Ennis had paced Bradon's office as she heard the two men discussing what to do, Kade keeping pace with her, his eyes on her face. She had stared down at him, not quite sure if she could trust him, but seeing the calm and steady look in his eyes, she had rested her hand on his head, a low whine coming from him as he pressed closer to him. Ennis didn't see Bradon's eyes on her at that point, his heart warming more towards her as he saw Kade's desperate attempt to make friends and to comfort her.

Bradon walked Will out and then returned to his office, leaning against a doorway, watching Ennis as she just stood, her arms wrapped around herself.

"Ennis?"

She spun, not having heard him return. "Bradon! You scared me! I didn't hear you."

"No, you didn't, but Kade did. If I had been a stranger, he would have been in front of you, pushing you backwards."

"Why?"

"Why? To protect you. He has decided you need his protection. I have seen that once or twice with him, but not to this extent."

"Branigan, I think it was, said it was because he saw you with me and that he decided I was family."

Bradon laughed. "That would be about it. Now, what do we do with you?"

"It's not just me anymore, Bradon. He's fixated on you as well."

He nodded. "I know he has. We'll not let him win. I can guarantee you that." He looked behind him. "Listen, tonight's when we have our weekly potluck."

"A weekly potluck? As in everyone in the building?" She stared at him, not quite sure she had heard him correctly.

"That's right. All of us. Anna and Doc started it just after we all moved her. And we are all from different parts of the country. And did we tell you we are all orphans?"

"No, you didn't. What's with that?"

Bradon shrugged. "It's what Barnabas felt led to to. We're all orphans. And we share initials."

"What? All of you?"

He laughed again. "All fourteen of us."

Ennis shook her head. "I don't see how he managed to accomplish that feat."

"He says it was God, and I must admit, I have to agree."

She just stared at him and then walked past him, his hand coming out to stop her.

"We won't keep you here, if you really do want to move somewhere else." His words were quiet.

She waited, before she looked at him, nodding. "I know that, Bradon. I feel safe here, probably for the first time in years. Even when I moved away, I wasn't safe. I just worry about Mom and Dad and Evan, what he'll do to them when he can't get to me."

"I talked to Barnabas, who talked to his father. They both met with your parents and Evan. There are plans in place for all of them."

"There are? Thank you." She moved away from him, heading for her own apartment, leaving him staring after her, a hand on Kade's head to keep him beside him, a low whine coming from the dog.

"I know, Kade. I know. You want to protect my lady, but she's not sure how she feels towards you. Give her time. She'll get there."

Chapter 9

A couple of hours later, Ennis stood, her eyes huge, as she watched the men mill around a board room, their voices teasing as they spoke with Anna and then Doc. She saw the three younger wives helping to set up the meal and suddenly felt out of place. Bradon was watching her from where he stood talking with Brady and Burnie before he excused himself and walked towards her.

"Ennis? Are you okay?"

His voice brought her head around and she stared at him, before she shook her head.

"No, I'm not. I don't belong here." She was gone before he could stop her, his feet carrying him after her.

"Ennis? Wait?" His hand stopped her forward movement. "If you don't want to stay, that's fine. At least come back and fill a plate. You can take it with you."

She stood, her arms wrapped around herself. "I can't, Bradon. I just can't." Tears clogged her throat and she ran, her apartment door closing behind her before she slid down and sat on the floor, her back to the door, tears raining down her face. Why, Lord? Why can't I stay? What do I fear so much? I could feel the fear intensifying in there, and I don't understand why.

Doc stood for a moment beside Bradon, before his hand rested on the younger man's shoulder and he prayed for his friend.

"I suspect she felt overwhelmed. Until you get to know us all, we can have that effect."

"I know, Doc. I know that, but there's something else. She found a picture of the two on us on her car today, and then we spoke with Will. I think she's just too tired to do this. I shouldn't have pushed her." Bradon stood, not sure if he should go after her or not.

"Let her have some time, then, Bradon." Doc looked behind him, seeing Anna standing there. "Anna will go talk with her, take her some food. Come on. Back in here with you. You need to eat too."

Anna watched as Bradon finally nodded and returned to the room, dishing up a plate, but not eating much. She sighed. Why, Lord? Why do these young men go through this with their ladies? She spoke quietly to Doc before fixing a plate and heading to find Ennis.

Ennis stood for a moment, studying Anna before she stepped back enough for Anna to enter. Anna's hands set the plate down in the kitchen before her arms swept Ennis into a hug, surprising her.

"Ennis? What can I do for you?" Anna stepped back, her eyes on the younger woman.

"End this? I really don't know, Anna. I'm sorry. I shouldn't have left."

"No, you should have. They all understand. They've all been there. Except that Berneen and Cadee were married, and Devaney was engaged, although she tried hard to not remember that."

"They belong. I don't. I'm only here until that monster is caught." Ennis turned to the counter, pulling the plastic wrap from the plate, and then just standing, staring down at it.

Anna sighed. Well, Lord, I guess it's up to You and I, isn't it?

"Ennis, I don't think you've picked up on something from Bradon, or if you have, whether you're ready to hear what he has to say. He has never done this before. He has shown no interest in any young lady, and there has been interest on their part. He has taken a step with you that we never thought to see him take. He wants to keep you safe. And I would gather once you are, he'll be speaking with you. I can see the interest he has in you, as a special young lady."

Ennis shook her head. "He shouldn't. He'll get hurt." She sighed, her eyes sliding closed. "He already has been. This monster is brutal. He'll go after Bradon. I know that."

"That's what he's done all along, isn't it? You've never been able to date, to see if one of the men in your circle of friends might be God's plan for you."

"You understand, Anna. How could I?"

Anna's arm was there, drawing Ennis to the living room and down on the couch, her voice raised in prayer for the younger woman. When she was finished, she sat, her eyes closed for a few minutes before she looked at Ennis.

"Draw your strength from the Lord, Ennis. Even when you go through the battle you are just entering, He is there, every step of the way. He does not wish for you to be beaten down. He wants you to overcome through His strength."

Chapter 10

Looking up from his desk at the canine compound he worked at, Bradon frowned as he heard footsteps heading his way. He was to have been on his own, Kade in a kennel in the training room, and he was sure he had locked the door. He didn't recognize the steps and rose, heading for the door, stopping suddenly as he saw the two men standing just outside his door.

"How can I help you two fellows?" Bradon's arms were crossed against his chest. "And perhaps you can explain how you got in, when the door was locked?"

Jason Lloyd stared at him, a scornful look on his face. "Doesn't matter. Just leave her be. Let her go home."

"Who would that be?"

"You know. That woman. Ennis. She's mine, not yours. Let her go back home."

Bradon shook his head. "You see, there's the issue. She doesn't belong to you. Never has. Never will. And as far as telling her where she is to live, I leave that decision to her. She's made her own plans. And they don't include you."

He didn't see the sudden movement of the second man until he felt the man's fist drive deep into his abdomen, doubling him over. He barely felt the blows that followed, leaving him in a crumpled heap

—

on the floor before the two men walked away. He didn't hear Kade frantically trying to get out of his kennel to get to Bradon.

Dallas had met up with Branigan and concerned enough, they had set out to find Bradon. Touching the door to the building, Branigan frowned.

"Bradon said he'd be here on his own. The door is always locked if there is only one person here." Branigan pulled it open, heading for where he could hear Kade. "Something's up for Kade to be that upset. What's wrong, boy?" He reached to unfasten the kennel, Kade shoving against the door and then racing for Bradon's office, the two men staring after him before they followed on a run.

Kade was down on his belly, his nose and tongue frantically moving to try and rouse Bradon. Branigan's voice pulled him back from his owner and Dallas dropped to his knees, before he spun.

"He's been beaten, Branigan, and badly. Call it in, and then stay with him." Dallas was on his feet, his eyes searching for anything. "How long would he have been on his own?"

"It's hard to say. I would have to speak with Rick, his employer."

"Let me have the number and I'll call. It's officially our investigation now." Dallas watched as the paramedics worked on Bradon before he turned to the patrol officers who were searching the area. "Branigan? Where would we find Ennis?"

Branigan shrugged as he glanced at his watch. "She's usually done about this time. Bradon's been driving her back and forth." He groaned. "And he can't today, and she'll be frantic."

"Head over and bring her to the hospital. She needs to be there." Dallas had turned before he saw the look on Branigan's face.

Ennis stood on the sidewalk in front of her work, her hands covering her mouth, as she stared at Branigan before he had her tucked into his truck.

"How bad?" She could barely get the words out.

"I don't know. They were still working on him when Dallas sent me to find you." He pulled to a stop outside the Emergency Department. "Ennis, wait. You can't just walk in there."

Ennis stared through the windshield, knowing Branigan was right. "I know, Branigan. But he's likely hurt because of me." She spun on the seat, a horrible thought coming to her mind. "Kade?"

"He was in a kennel, so not harmed." Branigan sighed. "We'll have to deal with him."

"I'll take him." Her words were fierce, even as her brows lowered. "I'll take him. He knows me. He needs me." She blinked rapidly to clear her eyes of tears. "And God help me, I need him."

Branigan nodded, his eyes on her. "Let's get you in. Doc's working today, so maybe that might help."

He slipped from the truck, walking around to open her door, his hand reaching for hers as they walked in. Sitting where she could see the doors, Ennis ignored the foot traffic around her, instead concentrating on calming herself. Branigan watched her closely before he pulled out his phone, turning it over and over, not wanting to call Barnabas. No, Breck, he thought. Barnabas was away for a couple of days with his parents.

"Breck?" Branigan could hear the sound of waves in the background and knew that Breck was on their beach. "It's Bradon."

"Bradon? What happened?" Breck walked quickly back towards the building, knowing something had happened.

"I'm not too sure what happened. Dallas and I went to meet him. We found him beaten and unconscious."

"He's still out?"

"He is. Kade was in his kennel but frantic to get to him."

"I see." Breck waved Blair over, his hand covering his phone for a moment as he explained what was going on. Blair nodded, heading on a run for the building. This is when the guys all came together, Breck thought. "He's in Emergency?"

"He is. Dallas sent me for Ennis. She's almost as frantic as Kade."

"Kade? Yes, Kade. Which one of us takes him?" Breck waved at Brady as he saw the men heading for their vehicles, the four women with them.

"Ennis."

"I'm sorry. I must have heard you wrong. I thought you said Ennis would." Breck's foot on the accelerator keep the truck at the speed limit on the highway until he slowed to turn into town.

"I did. Ennis has said she will take him. She is adamant on that, Breck, said he needed her." Branigan paused in his pacing, his eyes on Ennis. "She made an interesting comment."

"And that would be?" Breck threw his truck transmission into park and slipped from the seat, the doors locked after himself as he headed for the hospital door

"She said she needed him."

"She did." Breck watched as Branigan turned towards him, pocketing his phone. "Any word?"

"Not yet. It's been about thirty minutes."

"Doc's here?"

"He is." Branigan pointed to the chairs beside Ennis, sitting there, startling her.

"Branigan? Any word?" She was desperate to hear that Bradon would be walking out, but she knew better.

"Not yet." Branigan exchanged a glance with Breck. "They'll come find us."

"Kade?"

"Dallas said a patrol officer would take him to the Foundation building. The security guys will watch him until we can get you to him, or him to you."

She nodded, her eyes back on the door, her thoughts muddled, even as her hands clenched and unclenched against one another.

Chapter 11

Bradon's friends milled about the waiting room and then outside and back inside, worried about their friend.   No one had heard anything yet. Compassionate eyes sought and found Ennis, sitting huddled into a chair, her eyes glued to the door to the examination rooms. Anna sat on her one side, Meg on the other. Blair had called her parents. Her brother and father were around somewhere, they knew.

Will watched her for a moment before he spoke quietly to Dallas, heading for the examination rooms. They needed to talk to Bradon, but from what Dallas had said, Will knew that would have to wait. They had pulled security video feed but it hadn't helped in their investigation.

Doc stepped back from the stretcher, his eyes on Bradon. I prayed that he would not be hurt, Lord, but he is. How bad, we're not even sure yet. He turned as he heard footsteps and found Will and Dallas beside him, wincing at the bruising and blood they hadn't had a chance to clean away.

"Doc?"   Will's voice was low, his eyes troubled.

"I can't give you much yet, Will. Dallas. But I would say whoever did this knew what they were doing. He not likely had a chance to defend himself."

"No defensive wounds then?"

Doc shook his head at Dallas' question. "None that I can see. His hands are clean. There is some bruising and at least one finger is fractured, but nothing to indicate he defended himself."

"Sucker punched." Dallas drew in a deep breath. "What can you tell us?"

"We're sending him for imaging studies. We'll know more then." Doc turned, a frown on his face, his mouth opening and then closing. "We know there are internal injuries. His abdomen is very tender. The ribs may be fractured. Imaging will show that."

"You're looking at surgery?" Will shook his head, knowing that was a real possibility.

"We may be. The surgeon on call is heading this way. He'll let us know. At the very least, we suspect a pneumothorax, a collapsed lung. That means a chest tube." Doc turned back. "Ennis?"

"She's in the waiting room. Both Anna and her mom are with her." Will shook his head, a small smile cracking through the grimness on his face. "She is insisting on taking Kade."

"She is? That's interesting. I wouldn't have thought that." Doc pointed to the door. "Who do I talk to? I know Barnabas is away."

"I've spoken with him. He said he'd fax authorization through to let you talk to Ennis." Will pushed through the doors, pausing as he saw Ennis on her feet, heading his way, desperation in her movement.

"Doc?" She hugged him back as he swept her into a hug. "Bradon?"

<hr>

58

"He is still unconscious." Doc's arm tightened on her as he turned her back to her chair. "We're still assessing him, taking imaging pictures. The surgeon on call is on his way in."

Ennis sank into her chair, watching as he sat beside her, Anna moving to let him. She didn't feel her mother's arm around her. "All that? I didn't know it would be that bad." She looked up at Will. "Who did this?"

Will shook his head, pointing to Dallas. "He's the one working on it. He'll keep you updated." He glanced at his watch. "I'm sorry, Ennis. I have a meeting I need to get to. We'll speak."

Her eyes were back on Doc. She was desperate to see Bradon. Needed to, she thought.

"Can I see him?"

Doc watched her, knowing that Barnabas would have made that same decision, and sent through authorization for just that contingency. "Barnabas is his next of kin. Don't worry, Ennis. He'll let you in."

"But he's not here! How can he?" She was becoming frantic and then was on her feet, pushing through the men, heading for the outside. She needed to be away from everyone. She didn't see Jason waiting just outside the door, his hands reaching to stop her before he pulled them back, his angry eyes on Brady and Brennen as they moved in on either side of her.

Ennis paced, the two men keeping step with her, others of the men standing around, their eyes watchful. Dallas stood as well, his eyes not on Ennis but on Jason as he ran from the area.

"That's him!" Dallas' voice broke through Branigan's thoughts. "That's the man we want."

Dallas was running after him, Branigan on his heels as he took in what had been said. They slid to a stop, not finding him, before, frustration evident, they walked back towards Ennis, finding her just standing still, tears on her cheeks, Buckley standing in front of her.

Branigan frowned before he motioned to Brady, who walked slowly towards him.

"Brady?" He studied first Brady and then Ennis.

"They're taking him to surgery, Branigan. The surgeon sent Doc out to talk to her. They need to stop some bleeding and then put in a chest tube. He has a collapsed lung."

Branigan's eyes slid shut. It was what he had expected but had hoped he had been wrong. "They'll get Ennis in to see him?"

"They don't have time. Doc said he was being rushed up there as he was out here speaking with us." He looked past Branigan towards the edge of the parking lot. "What was that all about?"

"That monster, as Bradon puts it, was here. If you two hadn't been with her, she'd have been gone."

Brady paled. "He was that close?"

"He was. Dallas spotted him. I'll make sure we all get photos of him and anyone who is known to associate with him. I pray we can keep her safe."

Brady nodded as he watched Ennis move back inside, Doc's hand under her arm. "She's taking it hard. Where do they stand?"

Branigan shrugged, even as he studied the men gathering around them. "I don't think she knows yet. Bradon? I would say he's found his lady."

"That's exactly how he's acting." Brendon spoke quietly. "I'm heading for the chapel. I know, Buckley, you've set the prayer chain to work."

"I have. I'll be there shortly." Buckley stood for a moment, watching his friends walk away, before his eyes raised to the sky. "Lord, we could use Your healing powers for these two. Bradon's spoken to me, a bit, about what Ennis has gone through. She needs that touch of the garment, to help her overcome what is in her past, before she can move forward. Thank you for opening her heart to Kade. None of us saw that coming, but You did."

Chapter 12

Ennis paced the surgical floor waiting room, not willing to sit, not willing to leave, her thoughts muddled as to what Bradon actually meant to her. She had become accustomed to his being in her life. She had a good idea, she thought, of where he wanted to take their friendship, but she had been hesitant, not willing for him to be hurt. Sighing, Ennis acknowledged to herself that Bradon had become important to her. She was afraid for him right now, afraid that he wouldn't come back to her, that his life would be drastically altered because of the beating he had taken at the hands of that monster. She refused to call him by name. That gave him too much importance, and Ennis decided then and there she would bring him down, somehow, somewhere. Her life had been consumed by him for too long.

Meg watched as her daughter paced, knowing Ian and Evan were around somewhere, Ian likely in the chapel. Evan, she had last seen with Baird and Berneen and Berneen's brother, Darby. Where they had ended up, she had no idea. She rose, her arm around her daughter, drawing her down to a chair, a prayer raising in her heart for how much she was hurting.

"Mom? Why?"

"Why what, dear?"

—

"Why is he like he is? Can't he just leave me alone?" Ennis blinked rapidly, tears too near the surface, tears she refused to shed.

"Who? Jason? It's the sin in him that drives him. He knows no other way." Meg's head tilted as she saw Ian sit beside Ennis. "Your father has been doing some research, as he put it, into Jason's family."

Ennis jumped as she heard her father's voice and turned to face him. "Dad?"

"I wish I had done this years ago, lass. Maybe we won't be sitting here having this conversation. But then again, maybe we would be. Only the good Lord knows that for sure." He sighed, his eyes sliding closed for a moment. It was late evening by now, and they were still awaiting word on Bradon. "I've spoken with Will and that detective, Dallas. I've found information on him that was shoved under the carpet and hidden."

"Did you, Dad? Will this stop him?" Ennis' voice was low, cautious, hopeful, but doubt filled her that they could stop him.

"It's much worse than we ever knew, Ennis. The Lord has protected you in a way I never imagined. I won't go into details right now, but we will talk. I want Will or Dallas in on it. And likely Barnabas."

Her face whitening even more, Ennis could feel the fear rising within her. "Dad?"

"It's that bad and worse, Ennis. I can see how God protected you, even moving you away. Why you returned at this particular point in time? Only He knows, but we do need to take steps to keep you safe."

"Work?"

Ian nodded. "Your work. You can't be out and about right now." He shared a look with Meg. "Branigan talked to me earlier. Jason was here. When you went outside and the two fellows walked with you, he was ready to take you then."

Ennis drew in a deep breath. Her parents didn't think she could pale anymore than she had but she did. "I guess I won't be working then." She blinked rapidly once more, refusing to cry. "I'll have to call the office in the morning." She looked up at a sound from her father. "Dad? What did you do?"

"I didn't. It was that young detective. He's way ahead of me in this. He spoke with your employer, explained the situation. He agreed your safety was more important than you come in. He said he valued you as a trusted employee and wanted you to stay safe so you could come back to work."

She nodded. "I know I can't be there. It brings too much danger to them as well." Her eyes strayed to the door to the operating suite. "When will we hear about Bradon?"

Ian and Meg exchanged another look, Meg's look helpless even as Ian drew in a deep breath.

"Ennis?" He waited until she looked at him. "I'm going to ask you a question that I want you to think seriously about. And pray about. Bradon has stepped in as a friend and defender. I can see how he looks at you, just from the little time we've spent with him. I would hazard a guess he feels strongly he has found his lady, his heart, the one he wants to spend his life with." He paused, knowing that this was a conversation the younger couple should be having, without his interference, but given the danger they both found themselves in, he felt he had to step in. To counsel his beloved daughter. To ensure that she thought through and prayed over what decisions she would need to make. "I know you, lass. I see the stress and worry you're under. If he is the one that God has led to complete your life, we welcome him. If he's not, then we pray God protects your hearts, both of you."

Ennis nodded. When she spoke, her voice was barely audible. "Thank you, Dad, Mom. I know you have been praying over this, and that you won't have spoken, Dad, unless you felt strongly that God meant you to." She looked up at the ceiling, gathering her thoughts, as much as she could. "I don't know how I feel. I mean, I'm so grateful he has stepped in. I hurt because he was hurt on my behalf. As to the future, I don't see it clearly enough to answer."

Ian nodded. "That's what I was picking up, then, lass. Pray over it. I know Bradon is waiting for you to do that. It may come that he will speak to you before this is over. All we ask is that you listen and then pray. Seek counsel where you need to. With your Mom. With me. With Anna or Doc. With Buckley as your pastor. And better yet, with those three young ladies I see waiting for you to open up to them. I understand they have been through something similar. They will have counsel and advice for you."

Chapter 13

On her feet, Ennis moved towards the surgeon as he walked her way. He studied her and nodded. Doc was right. She's invested in Bradon. And I know Bradon from church. He would be doing his best to protect her.

"Doctor?" Ennis could barely speak, seeing the fatigue and grim look on the surgeon's face.

"Let's sit, Ennis. I'm Dr. Walter Wilson. I've just finished with your young man. I stayed in Recovery with him until we transferred him to an ICU bed." He sank down, grateful to be sitting.

"Doctor? How is he?"

"He's alive. God had his hand on him, Ennis, make no doubt about that. He could very easily have died. Dallas and Branigan found him in time." He watched her face closely. "I spoke with Barnabas. He asked that I add you to Bradon's medical records as next of kin." He smiled at her look of surprise. "Bradon thinks of you that way, I'm told."

She shrugged, her eyes looking everywhere but at Walter. "I guess. I don't know him well enough to know what he thinks."

Walter grinned at her. "I know Bradon. He thinks that way. I've been told a bit of what he did. He's interested in you. Explore your friendship with him." He sighed. "As to his injuries?"

Ennis searched his face. "Doctor?"

"Call me Walter. We share a church, so no formality. Now, as to his injuries. He has two broken fingers on his right hand. Fractured ribs. One of them did puncture the lung. I would say he was kicked there. We've inserted a chest tube to aid that. He had bleeding internally. He has lost his spleen. The kidneys were bruised. The liver had a laceration. We've fixed him up as best we can. He's in God's hands, Ennis." He stood, reaching for her hand and drawing her to her feet. "Come. Let's get you to your fellow. Once you've seen him, I want you to go home and get some sleep." He nodded towards the waiting room. "There will be some of the fellows here all night. But they have all spoken to Doc. They want you safe and that means back at the building."

She sighed. "In other words, I just accumulated more guardians. Two weren't enough?"

Walter laughed as he led her towards Bradon. "Just keep in mind there is a lot of equipment and lines running to his body. He is sedated. We had to do that."

Ennis nodded, knowing what he wasn't saying. "I get that. Can I see him, please?"

She stood, her hands covering her mouth, seeing the deepening colouring of the bruising against his white face, the shadow of a beard there. She reached to touch his face, tears flowing that she angrily swiped at. Ennis prayed for his healing and that Jason would be found before anyone else was hurt. She knew him well enough to know that would happen. He was like that.

Finally turning away at a touch on her arm, she was wrapped in her father's arms, silent sobs shaking her body before he led her from the room and to his vehicle, heading for her home. He knew Breck had ensured someone from the Foundation was with them. He just didn't know that all of the men were there, their vehicles surrounding his, to ensure that Bradon's lady was safe before some headed back for the ICU, intent on taking turns to be there for their friend.

Ennis stood inside her door, her eyes on Kade, who stood, waiting for her to speak. Dropping to her knees, she swept him into a hug, his tongue licking at her face before he looked past her, searching for Bradon.

Early the next morning, Ennis had finally stretched out to sleep, her sleep broken by dreams. Kade had stood, his chin on the bed, his eyes on her before he cautiously crept up beside her, tight to her back, his chin on her neck, knowing he wasn't allowed on the bed, but this time, he just had to. His master's lady needed comfort and he couldn't do that from the floor.

Chapter 14

Two days later, Ennis stood at Bradon's bedside, watching as he moved restlessly. He had been moved to a regular hospital bed, and that encouraged her, but also frightened her. It would be so much easier for someone to get to him here, she thought, even though she knew there was a police officer stationed outside his door for now, just until Dallas could talk to him.

Ennis wanted him to wake up, to ensure her that he was recovering, and that he didn't blame her. On the other hand, she didn't want him to wake, to blame her, to tell her to leave, that he didn't want to see her again. That was her fear, she decided, and then took that fear to the Lord. Whatever is Your will, she thought.

She finally walked away, knowing she needed to, nodding at Evan as he rose from his seat in the waiting room, his arm out to hug his sister. She didn't see Dallas waiting to speak with her, her eyes blinded with tears. Dallas stared at her and then towards Bradon's room, moving that way, nodding at the officer on guard before he pushed open the door, his feet taking him to stand where Ennis had just been standing. He didn't believe in God, but seeing how much trust these new friends of his had in God, he was starting to question that.

Dallas stood, watching as Bradon roused and searched the room. He's looking for Ennis, he thought, and she's not here.

—

"Bradon?"

Bradon's head shot around, and his eyes closed as the vertigo hit. His stomach roiled before he could control it. His eyes opened to see a contrite Dallas watching him, his hand on the call button.

"Dallas? Is that you?" Bradon's voice was rough.

"It is. I called your nurse."

"Why?"

"Why what?"

"Why would you call me a nurse? Where am I?"

"You're in the hospital, Bradon. We need to talk." Dallas stepped to one side as the nurse approached. "Sylvie?"

"Yes, Detective? I see he's awake. That's good." She assessed him, taking his vitals, and then standing watching him. "Bradon?"

Bradon carefully moved his head to look at her. "The room's spinning. I don't think it should be."

"Vertigo. Dr. Wilson was afraid of that. I'll put a call in to him. He's somewhere here in the hospital."

Bradon watched her walk away, before his attention turned to Dallas. "What did I go and do? And please, don't move. Stay in one spot."

Dallas gave a low laugh. "I can do that." He set his portfolio down and reached for a chair. "How's this?"

"That's better." Bradon's eyes closed. "Tell me. What happened?" His eyes popped open. "Ennis?"

"She's fine, Bradon. In fact, she left not too long ago. We've had to make her leave. Barnabas has been adamant about that." He grinned. "Besides, she has to look after Kade, did you know that?"

"What?" Bradon stared at him. "She doesn't like dogs. Why would she be looking after Kade?"

Dallas shrugged. "She was adamant that she took Kade. Said he needed her." He frowned. "She also said she needed him. Does that make sense?"

The other man frowned in turn, and then laid his head back. "It does make sense. She's terrified of dogs, but Kade is just moving in on her, not letting her back away. I would say she's made a connection with him, and he with her."

"That happens, does it?" Dallas stared at Bradon for a moment before he reached for his note pad. "We need to get your statement, Bradon, before anyone else talks to you. Can you tell me what happened?"

"Jason did. He and another man appeared in the building. The door was locked, so I have no idea how they made it in. I was focused on Jason, telling him that they needed to leave when I was sucker punched. I don't remember anything after hitting the floor." He sighed and then grimaced with pain, finding it difficult to draw a deep breath. His hand hit the chest tube and he frowned once more.

"The other man beat you up. Did a good job on it. Walter went in and repaired the damage. He'll be around to talk to you." Dallas looked down at his notes and then back at Bradon. "You won't be working for a while, I can tell you that. And Ennis is not working, either. Jason was waiting outside the doors to the Emergency Department. If two of your friends hadn't been there, she would be gone." He looked back at the door. "And her father has been doing some digging into this man. He's provided information that should have been found before."

Bradon stared at the IV dripping through the line to the back of his hand. "I was getting some stuff on him. He's not a nice person." He turned to Dallas, his eyes closing until the vertigo eased. "How do we do this? How do we keep her safe? He'll be watching her. When she comes here. When she goes home. Around our building. And that can be a problem, around the building. They can get in there as well."

"We know that, Bradon. Breck and I have talked, as have Branigan and I. We're working on keeping her safe. All your friends have come to me at some point, volunteering to help. Anna and the three younger ladies have been adamant they won't be left out. And then we have her family."

"And that's going to be a problem. If he can't get to her, he'll go after one of them. I would suspect her mother, but her father or even Evan will be targeted." Bradon's voice died away as he thought it through. "Kade can't stay with her all the time. I need to find a dog for her."

"She won't take one." Dallas grinned at the frown on Bradon's face. "She has already told me that. I asked her."

Bradon sighed. "There goes that idea. What ideas do you have?" He stared at Dallas when he stated his preference. "That's not happening."

Chapter 15

Bradon stared at the thirteen men, no, fourteen, he corrected himself as Evan slipped into the room, three days later as they stood, arms folded across their chest, grim looks on their faces.

"I can so leave." Bradon didn't shake his head, knowing the vertigo would be there. "I have my discharge papers."

"That may well be. But, where do you go? You can't stay on your own for a few days. Anna and Doc are away. The rest of us are working." Breck spoke for the group.

"He can come stay with us." They all turned as a group as Evan spoke up. "That's why I'm here. Ennis sent me. She wants Bradon to go stay with Mom and Dad."

Breck pulled his mouth down as his head bobbed from side to side, a small smile lurking in his eyes. He met the eyes of all the other men, seeing their relief and agreement.

"Okay, so you're off to stay with Meg and Ian." Barnabas nodded. "That's good. You won't get away with trying too much too soon."

Bradon stared first at Barnabas, then at Evan, frowning as he saw the faint hint of mischief on Evan's face. "Does Ennis know?"

"Does Ennis know what?"

His eyes slid closed as Ennis made her way through the group of men, who parted to let her in.

"Bradon? Do I know what?" When he didn't answer, she spun to study each man, stopping with her eyes on her brother. The men watched in fascination at the silent battle of wills between the siblings, Evan with a grin on his face.

"Mom asked that Bradon stay with them for a few days. He can't be on his own, and Doc said he and Anna were away on a planned holiday." Evan reached for his sister, drawing her into a hug. He kept his voice low enough so only she could hear when he spoke. "It's okay, sis. If you don't want that to happen, I can stay with him at his place. Mom just thought it might be easier for him to be with them."

She nodded as she hugged him back. "I wondered if she would. It's fine." She stepped back, her eyes on his face, before she spoke. "Bradon, Mom has spoken. She does want you to stay with them. In case you missed it the other time, she's a retired nurse."

"That's perfect." Brady spoke, a grin on his face. "Then we don't have to worry about him."

"You do." Evan laughed at their looks and the glare from Bradon. "Her cooking is excellent. We can't let him eat much." Then a look of horror crossed his face. "I forgot."

"You forgot what?" When Evan remained silent, Brennen spoke again. "What did you forget?"

"Kade. Ennis doesn't like dogs."

Ennis watched with amusement the looks of consternation on the men's faces as they frantically tried to come up with a different plan, her eyes finally settling on Bradon, who sat in the wheelchair, fully dressed and ready to leave, seeing the smile lurking in his eyes.

"Who? Kade? Of course he comes. He's not a dog." Ennis reached to push the chair forward, leaving stunned silence in her wake.

"What did she just say?" Benen walked after her.

"That Kade wasn't a dog?" Blair followed, as they did other men.

"Guys?" When they turned, Evan spoke. "She's made her peace with Kade. He's won her over, proving that dogs can be gentle. She will still fear other dogs, but not him."

They shared a look and then nodded. Evan had stated just what Ennis had shown them.

An hour later, Bradon sank down with relief into a wing back chair, his eyes closing for a moment as his head spun. He jumped slightly as he felt a cool hand on his forehead, and then hands tucking a blanket around him. He slept, no seeing Meg standing watching him, her arm around Ennis before she turned her daughter to the kitchen.

"I know this isn't what you wanted or planned, dear." She moved around the kitchen, making tea for them, checking on her meal in the oven, before she sat, her hand reaching to still her daughter's restless one.

"No, it's not, Mom." Ennis stopped, her emotions in a roil. "He could have been killed, and it would have been my fault."

"Not your fault, Ennis. Never your fault. And he would not and will not walk away from you. That is a given, as you say." Meg watched her daughter closely, seeing how emotional she was. "It's not easy, dear. Not when you fall in love and aren't sure if the other person feels that way."

"How do I do this, Mom? I can't let him see that." Ennis buried her face in her hands.

"You go on as you have. Taking care of him. Taking care of yourself. And taking care of Kade." Meg smiled down as Kade stood with his chin on Ennis' lap. "Kade has made you his duty, you know."

"I know he has. He was like this before Bradon was hurt." Ennis' hand rubbed at Kade's head. "But how do we end this?"

"Dallas is working on it, Will said. He can't say what has been found or what evidence they have. He did say Dallas wanted to talk to you two when Bradon was able to." She rose as she heard a tap at the door and returned, Barnabas behind her.

"Barnabas? Why are you here? What happened?" Ennis was beginning to panic.

"It's okay, Ennis. I just stopped by to make sure you two were fine and to offer any help we can. The guys are working through what happened. I think you'll find they'll dig up information even Dallas can't."

"They are? They will? But that's not what they do."

"It's what they do for their friends, and they consider you a friend." Barnabas' look was compassionate. "They see how Bradon is with you and how you are with him. They want to do this for you two." He paused, his eyes on Ian as he entered through the back door. "Branigan and Brendon want to talk to you. Benen is searching for whatever information he can find on the internet. The others are talking to your friends, Bradon's friends, searching for this person."

"But how do they know who my friends are? I never told them." Ennis was puzzled at his words.

"All they had to do was come to your town, ask a couple of questions, and the list of people wanting to talk to them just grew on its own."

"It did? Okay, I guess. I just pray they find him and soon. He's taken enough of my life." Ennis was on her feet, moving for the living room, Kade pacing at her side, his head turned up to watch her.

"One would never have known she is scared of dogs, seeing her and Kade." Ian's voice was quiet as he spoke.

"No, you won't. Kade has done wonders for her." Meg rose, pulling her meal from the oven. "Barnabas, you'll stay for a meal?"

"I will and thank you, Meg."

—

Chapter 16

A week later, Bradon sat carefully into his chair in his office at the building, sighing as he did so. He felt better, but also worse, if that made any sense. Kade was pacing restlessly, and he watched him, a smile coming to his face. *He's missing Ennis, isn't he? Lord, I don't know where I'm going with this lady, or where this adventure will take us. All I know is I love her, and want her to stay in my life for as long as You allow. But this has to be from You. I can't run ahead of you.*

He looked towards the door as he heard a tap and then Branigan entered, followed by Baird, Benen, Blair and Brady. *My team,* he thought, aware of how Barnabas had divided the men into two teams of six, thinking this worked for fostering their growth in God and sometimes when he needed to send men into a situation.

The men seated themselves, passing around their coffee, before Bradon spoke.

"I take it you're here for prayer and then a conference."

They all grinned and nodded. They broke up into twos, spending time in prayer, before they gathered once more.

Bradon searched his friends' faces, knowing that they would support him in whatever it was he decided to do. Just what that was, though, he was uncertain of.

"What are your plans?" Baird spoke first.

"My plans? Right now, I don't have any other than not falling over when I stand up." Bradon's hand rubbed at his temple. "Did that even make any sense?"

"It does." Brady spoke up, the paramedic in the group. "You took a hard few blows, Bradon. We know you had a concussion. That beating could have killed you, but didn't. You'll live with the vertigo and learn how to handle it."

"That's what I'm afraid of. That I have to live with it. It can affect my work." His eyes slid closed as he tried to imagine not doing what he had always done.

"Doc said he talked to a chiropractor friend who is willing to see you. He's had good success treating conditions like yours." Brady continued to watch his friend, concern on his face.

"Now, what about Ennis? And what's going on with her?" Bradon searched his friends' faces once more, seeing the concern but also the determination to solve this mystery. "How close are we to finding him?"

"That we don't know, but he's a nasty bit of work, from all that we're finding out." Benen held up a folder. "I have given a copy of everything we've managed to track down, including the names of other victims."

"Other victims?" Bradon's voice stopped, horror in his heart. "There have been other victims?"

—

Blair nodded, a grim look on his face. "There have been. Young ladies. Teenagers." He paused, his eyes on Bradon as Bradon made the connection. "You're right in what you're thinking. Human trafficking. As to what he wants with Ennis, we think it has now turned to revenge. She escaped him, and no one does that. That's what we're hearing on the street."

"And I can gather, she won't be walking away from him if he gets his hands on her." Bradon sat back, his hand idly rubbing at Kade's ears. "How do we keep her safe?"

"That's what we been discussing. We didn't mean to behind your back, Bradon." Branigan spoke up. "We've been able to talk to other ladies who escaped him. Between us all, we spoken to probably a dozen. What they have in common is that they have a significant other, a boyfriend, a husband. You catch the drift?"

Bradon's eyes were on Branigan, the leader of their group. "I do. Once someone takes over their protection, he backs away. But I don't think he will with her."

"No, I don't think he will. He's proven that when he came after you. You two are not a couple, at least as far as we know. All that has happened is that you have been seen with her. That was enough to set him off. If your relationship deepens, it will only get worse for you."

"That's what we're afraid of. We talked over the last week, on our own, with Evan, with her parents. Barnabas. Will. Dallas. We just didn't talk to you guys, but I have a pretty good idea what you're thinking." He smirked at the looks on their faces. "I mean, after all, three of us have married. But I won't do that to Ennis. Not unless it's a last ditch effort. She's not ready for that. I don't know that she ever will be."

"She's interested, Bradon." Benen spoke up. "She's interested but she won't say anything. Not until you do. And even then, if this is not resolved, she'll walk away. She doesn't want you hurt anymore than you have been."

"That's right." Branigan eyed his friend. "No one else saw her when I went to get her that day. It almost destroyed her, Bradon, to think that a friend had been hurt because of her."

Bradon nodded. "I know. She's talked to me about that." He didn't see the looks of surprise on the others' faces. "She's been upfront with me. We're talking about where we want to go." He paused, biting at his lower lip, not quite sure how much to say.

Chapter 17

Pacing her apartment, Ennis was growing tired of feeling like a captive. She sighed, knowing that she had to stay safe and right now that meant staying inside. But that wasn't her. She wanted to be out on her bike, to be running, to even walk the grounds. She grabbed her keys and headed for the lobby, standing staring outside.

She didn't see Bradon approaching her and jumped when he spoke from beside her. Turning, she studied him, seeing he was staring out the window, not looking at her. Kade nudged at her hand, and she laid it on his head.

"Feeling like you're a captive or in prison, sweetheart?"

"I am, Bradon. But I know if I go out there, it could mean my death or the death of someone with me. When does it end?" Ennis could feel the despair rising in her.

"Soon, I pray. But, for now, we can go out, as long as we stay close to the building. There are gardens with seats or paths we can walk." He reached for her hand, tugging her to the door and outside, Kade keeping pace.

Ennis walked beside him, watching him carefully.

"How are you feeling now, Bradon?"

"Better, thanks. The vertigo is getting less. I just need to be careful how I move. The chiropractor is working wonders with that."

"I'm so glad." She shivered. "When I first saw you, when Will took me in, I didn't think you would live. It was pretty brutal."

"That's what I'm told." He felt at his face, knowing the bruising was turning yellow and green. "I can live with what happened. But can you?"

She stopped, her hand rubbing at her face. "That I'm not sure of. Not anymore." She looked around, tugging him to a bench, and sitting, her eyes on the building in front of her. "I really hate him for this."

"I know you do. It's to be expected. It's our humanness that comes through in situations like this. It's how we let it affect us. That's what we need to take to God. I have had to."

"And what answers have you gotten? I know he's not done. I am sure he's here somewhere watching us or has someone watching us. How do we go about our normal lives?" She shifted on the bench so she could see his face. "How do you go back to your work?"

Bradon shrugged. He had talked to his employer and they were working on a schedule for him. He knew he wouldn't be travelling for a while and he could accept that. It was the training that would be affected. Right at present, he wasn't able to. That distressed him. They had both agreed he'd do assessments on buildings and people, and have the dogs they needed to assess brought to them. He would work on that when Rick was in the building.

"Rick and I have talked. We're working it out. I just don't get to travel. That's all." He watched her closely. "That's what I had done, you know. I had been away assessing dogs and stopped for a break that day."

"And if you hadn't, who knows where I would have been. Or even if I would still be alive." She wrapped her arms around herself, distress on her face. "I know what he does. He told me. That's what drove me away the first time. I had to stay safe to be able to stay here."

"He told you?" Anger grew in Bradon. "When?"

She shrugged. "When he first started all this. He told me he would sell me to someone."

Bradon's arms came around her, holding her as she wept. "I'm sorry, sweetheart. That shouldn't have happened." He paused, getting his anger under control, praying that God would stop this monster. "I'm sorry you've had to live with that."

She shrugged. "It's him. He's the one driving this." She paused, a thought running through her mind. "Can we use that to catch him?"

"What do you mean?" Bradon wasn't sure what she was saying.

"I mean, can we use his words to trap him? I know he has had to have help from the authorities. That's the only way he's been able to get away with this." She lifted her head, her eyes staring into the distance. "There has to be someone else involved, someone behind him. He doesn't have the smarts or the ability or the contacts to do what he's done." She sighed, sorrow on her face. "How many has he done this to? How many have disappeared, had their lives destroyed?"

"Dallas has said the same thing. He's digging into that and he has other police services doing the same. It's not a pretty picture they're finding." Bradon's arms tightened on her.

"I didn't think it would be. I just want this over."

"Me, too. But if it hadn't happened, I would not have met you." Bradon waited as she thought about his words and then turned to him. "I would not have wanted to missing having you in my life, Ennis. Not at all. We need to talk at some point. I'm not sure you're ready for that conversation yet."

She shrugged, her eyes telling him she was, her words asking for space. "I'm not sure, Bradon. I'm just not sure."

Chapter 18

Brady was on a search two days later. He had been handed a letter as he came out of a local business, the young boy running away before he could stop him. He had stared down at it, seeing Bradon's name printed in bold black letters.

Bradon turned at Brady's call, catching his balance as he shifted his weight, Kade leaning tight into him. Kade was torn, Bradon thought, amused for a moment at the distress that was causing Ennis. She didn't want him with her, stating he was Bradon's dog and needed to be with him, but at the same time, welcoming his attention.

"Brady? What's the rush?"

Brady waved the letter. "This. I was handed it by a young boy as I came out of the book shop. They are looking for you but can't get to you." He handed over the envelope. "I called Dallas. He wants you to wait to open it. He's on his way out."

"And Ennis will need to be here. She's with the other three ladies today. Something about baking or some such thing."

"Baking?" Brady's face lit up. "Will they share?"

"Of course we will." Ennis' voice behind him had him jumping and then spinning, catching the grin she was trying to hide, and then his eyes dropped to the container she kept shoving at him. "These are yours. I was headed for your place when I saw you pull in and head for Bradon."

"Thank you, Ennis. I'll catch up with the others later." Brady's face lit up with a smile before he sobered. "I was looking for Bradon, yes. And here's Dallas."

Dallas grinned at them. "And here I am. Brady, you have baking!"

"I do, and I'm not sharing." Brady laughed at the glum look on Dallas's face.

"I have some set aside for you and Will, Dallas." Ennis took pity on him. "We ladies wanted to say thanks. I'll grab it when we're through." She shivered as she looked around. "Can we go inside? I can feel him somewhere out there."

Bradon's arm was around her as he turned her towards the building. "We can. How be we head for your apartment? That way, Dallas can grab his goodies when he leaves."

Ennis made sure the men had their coffee before she excused herself, heading for her spare room and the paperwork she had dug up from years ago. She had hidden it away, making a trip home the day before to find it. Evan had found her staring down at it, an arm coming around her, his prayer in her ear before he asked what he could do. She had simply shaken her head, knowing he was talking to people, finding information he was passing on.

She stood just back from the kitchen doorway, watching the three men as they interacted, knowing they were waiting for her to return, but also knowing she was hesitant to. Something told her this day would change her life. She just wasn't sure how. Her eyes dropped to the folders, some of them thick. Evan had simply handed her his investigations and asked that she pass them on to either Dallas or Will.

Bradon's eyes raised as he sensed her near him and rose, coming to stand in front of her, shielding her from the others.

"Ennis?"

"This is hard, Bradon. This is so hard." She held up the folders. "I had stuffed some of these away, never wanting to look at them. I deliberately kept from remembering what I had. Maybe if I hadn't, you wouldn't have been hurt. And Evan has been busy as well."

"We'll let Dallas take this. He or someone he works with will go through it. They'll talk to you and Evan, I'm sure." His head bent to hers as he prayed, knowing his lady was hurting.

Dallas eyed the stack of folders that Ennis slid across the table at him. "This is what you've been doing lately."

"Some is Evan's work. He's been working the last few weeks on it." She sighed, a bleak look on her face, even as her face whitened. Brady watched her closely. "Some of it goes back to when it all started. I had forgotten what I had. I think I was shoving it all away, not wanting to see it. Not wanting to have to deal with him. And that has gotten us to this point." She poked at the letter Dallas had set down. "Aren't you going to open that?"

"We will, sweetheart. But first, you know what we do." He waited until she nodded. "Brady?"

"Of course." Brady's head bowed as he prayed for them, for what they would find, that it would advance the investigation to the point they could arrest Jason and whoever it was he was working for.

Dallas paused as he reached for latex gloves, his eyes on Ennis and then Bradon. When I open this, there is no going back. We don't know what this man is planning but my experience tells me it isn't good.

He slit open the envelope and pulled out the folded piece of paper, hesitating before he unfolded it, his eyes going to first Ennis and then Bradon before they stopped on Brady. He glanced down to read it, his face growing grim as he did so, taking in the words. He folded the paper back up and inserted it into the envelope again, no words coming from him.

Bradon and Ennis exchanged a glance before Bradon spoke.

"Dallas?"

Shaking his head, Dallas looked at him and then Ennis. "I can't or even won't show it to you. It's ugly. Bradon, your life has been threatened once more. You don't want to know what he's planning for you. We need to take even more steps to keep you safe. Ennis, we need you to stay here, in the building as much as you can. I know. I know. You want to be outside. Just make sure you have some of the men with you when you do. You can't be out there on your own or with just the ladies. He's made it very clear he intends to take you. He hasn't said what he plans, but the threat is there that you don't live."

Ennis, her face pale, had nodded. "That's what he's done along. Threatened that." She paused, biting at her upper lip. "What is triggering it now? It's not just because I'm home. He could have taken me when I was away."

"I think that you'll find it's partly you coming back to where he's been defeated." Brady studied her closely. "And you did defeat him. You managed to escape and make a life for yourself. Coming back here has triggered his anger towards you."

"I would say Brady is correct, Ennis. He likely feels that you are the one who got away and you did. He needs to rectify that. Seeing you with Bradon has triggered a deep-rooted anger in him. He wants both of you to pay. Bradon, you helped her escape and are keeping her safe. Ennis, you have escaped him many times on many levels. He can't accept that you have done so." Dallas paused to gather his thoughts. "He may also be getting pressure from whomever it is he is working for."

"I would think he would be." Ennis stood, pacing. "So, how do we do this? How do we catch them, but keep us safe? I don't want Bradon hurt again."

Chapter 19

Locking up after the men had left, Ennis cleaned the kitchen, her hand resting for a moment on the chair back where Bradon had sat, his hand reaching at times for her. She was beginning to depend on him in a way that she didn't depend on anyone and that scared her. Her heart lifted in prayer, asking for wisdom and guidance, before she headed for her computer.

She had signed up for a college course, planning on working on it in her spare time. She snorted. That's all she seemed to have, she thought. Spare time. Working in a medical office had been what she had thought she wanted to do. Now, she wasn't so sure. She had some money saved that would get her by until she was back at work, but she was torn. She didn't think she could go back.

Ennis stared at the computer monitor before she shut the computer back down. This wasn't what she wanted to do. Just what that was, she wasn't even sure. She just knew she was at loose ends and didn't like that feeling. She had never been like that.

Her phone chiming caught her attention and she reached to swipe her finger across the screen to wake it up. Pulling up her text messaging app, a soft smile covered her face. Bradon! Now, she wondered, how did he know she was feeling like she was?

Her fingers flying across the phone, she sent off an answer, and waited for his response. A soft laugh came from her as she saw the photo of Kade staring intently into the camera and then read the accompanying text. *I miss you, too, Kade, and I miss Bradon. How did that happen? How did he become such a part of my life.*

She thought through what she had given Dallas and sighed. He had a lot of work to do to confirm what she had noted, and she knew he would do his best. But would his best be good enough? Would he find Jason and his backer in time? Ennis knew that she was on borrowed time, that she would be found. She just prayed that Bradon was not with her when she was.

Bradon turned out his bedside light as he pulled the covers up over him, waiting for the spinning sensation in his head to stop. That always happened when he laid down or sat up, and he was getting frustrated. His thoughts too turned to the conversation they had had with Dallas and Brady. He wanted this over. Bradon wanted to explore the relationship with Ennis that was developing. He had covered it in prayer and felt confident enough to move forward.

He turned to his side, his hand reaching for Kade, knowing Kade was not to be on the bed, but Kade had had plans of his own, crawling up beside him to lie tight to him. Bradon frowned, and then smiled, knowing this is how Kade had reacted with Ennis. He didn't have the heart to tell Kade no, but he would have to at some point.

The next morning, Bradon walked back into his work, Kade pacing beside him, his face white and stern. He didn't find it easy coming back to where he had been assaulted, and his physicians had acknowledged to him, almost killed. That he was alive was God's hands, they told him.

Rick watched as Bradon moved through the building, Kade beside him, before he approached him.

"Bradon?"

"Rick? How do we stand for training?" Bradon went right to the point.

"We're good. I can use you in the office, sorting through our applications and security requirements. That you are good at, better than any of us. Just don't over do it." He looked down at Kade. "How's Kade?"

Bradon began to laugh, bringing a puzzled look to Rick's face. "Now, Kade. He's in love and doesn't want to leave his lady. It's Ennis. He's become her protector, wants to be with her."

Rick grinned. "Well then, do something about it." He walked away at Bradon's protest.

His protest dying in the air, Bradon looked down at Kade. "And I could, you know. I could ask her to marry me. I just don't think she's ready for something like that." He sighed, his hand reaching to rest on Kade. "Come on, boy. Let's find Sandy and see how much paperwork she has for us. I know it will be lots. And I can't work a full day. Not yet, anyway. But I could take some home and work from there, keeping Ennis with me. Now, there's a thought."

Ennis looked up as she heard her name, rising from the bench at the front of the building as Doc approached.

"Ennis. I haven't talked to you in a few days. How are you?" He reached to hug the younger woman.

"I have no idea, Doc. Everyone asks me that. I always say I don't know. Maybe I should come up with a new line." She grinned as he laughed.

"Now, there's the spirit. Just keep saying that. All our guys and ladies here understand. Your parents and brother as well. By the way, where is your brother?"

"Evan? I heard from him this morning. He was catching a flight to the Yukon. A trip he has planned for years."

"That's good. He's safe there?"

Ennis shrugged. "I have no idea. Are any of us safe right now?"

Doc studied her, seeing the fine lines that the stress and danger were working in her face. "I would pray that we are, but God may have other ideas for us and allow us to go through hard times. He has with you. I can see you working with the ladies and girls at the shelter. Have you thought about that?"

She stared at him. "How did you do that?"

"Do what?" Doc was puzzled.

"Give me a new line of work. I was looking for something." She sat back, her hands rubbing down her legs. "I have my psychology degree, but decided

I didn't want to use it. I wanted to be out in the medical office."

"And now, you're not sure you want to continue with that. All I can say is pray, Ennis. Ask God to show you. This may be why you've gone through what you have. We don't always know the plans God has for us, not until He is ready to show us."

She nodded. "I will do that, Doc. I was looking at a course I had signed up for. A business course and suddenly found I wasn't interested in it. I have resigned from it." She looked up at him. "How do you know the words to say? I've seen you do it with the others."

He shrugged. "God, Ennis. He gives me the words I need when I need them. That is how I have always prayed, you know. For Him to lead me as He will, that I might encourage someone else."

"Just like Barnabas encouraged Paul." She sat for a moment, her face thoughtful. "That's what Barnabas does, isn't it? He found the men God wanted here, to use them in the community, to do just that."

Doc smiled. "And you have gotten exactly what Barnabas and his father planned. Not many do until it is explained. They think it was just named after Barnabas."

Ennis shook her head. "God chose the name when Barnabas was born, and then led them on this journey. He has been needed greatly." She looked up at Doc again. "But where's his lady? He needs someone to encourage him."

"He has never said, Ennis. And I won't pry. If he wants you to know something, he tells you." Doc sat back, confident that Ennis really did understand his words.

Ennis sat for a moment before she rose, her thoughts muddled. She needed to speak with her mother, but then again she couldn't. She looked up to see Kade standing in front of her, eager for her attention, before she raised her eyes to Bradon, seeing a similar eagerness on his face, and walked towards him, into his arms and his hug. I have come home, she thought. I have come home to someone who loves me.

Chapter 20

Bradon watched Ennis closely as they walked back towards the building, her hand in his. Today, he sensed a change in her, she just seemed more open to him. Lord, I don't know what's going on, but You do. Thank you for this lady.

"Bradon?" Her voice caught at his attention, there was such a difference note to it.

"Yes, sweetheart?"

"Doc had an interesting comment." Her feet stopped, as she bit at her lip, Kade nudging her to move. "He said maybe I went through this, so I could help others. Would God do that?"

Bradon shrugged. "He could and He would. Depends on the person and where God wants them. But I can see that happening for you."

"You can? That's what Doc has said. I'm not sure on that." She moved forward, blowing out a breath, Bradon's eyes on her, a puzzled look on his face. "I guess I should tell you I have my psychology degree. I didn't want to use it. Didn't like that thought. But now, is that what God wants?"

"He will tell you when you're ready for that step. I'm guessing you don't want to work in the medical office again/"

She shook her head. "I thought I did, but now I'm finding I don't like it. It's not what I want to do." She stopped just inside the doors, her toe rubbing against the hardwood floor. "How do I tell my parents?"

"I think you'll find they understand and are expecting this." Bradon's arm around her drew her to one of the seating arrangements, Kade's chin on her knee as soon as she sat. "Your Dad mentioned that you really didn't fit the office, and why would you have chosen to do that?"

She looked up, surprise on her face. "Dad said that? He's never questioned me on it."

"And you'll find he wouldn't, not unless he really had to. And it's not to that point as yet." He looked around. "Now that you're not working, and I can't, what do we do to put in time?"

"Research. And more research. And road trips. We need to find this monster. He's not hiding, at least not very well. The last I heard from Evan before his flight took off was that Jason was seen in our hometown, right out in the open."

"And he will be. Legally at least. But morally? That is done to put the pressure on you, to make you afraid. He's hoping you make a mistake and he can grab you." Bradon's arm tightened around her. "And I don't want that to happen. I would miss you greatly if you disappeared. And so would Kade."

"Kade? He would?" She reached down to rub at Kade's back, a blissful expression on the dog's face at her touch. "He's something else, you know. I am afraid of dogs, but he just walked right in and took over."

Bradon laughed at her comment, even as he saw Branigan and Brendon heading their way. "He knew you needed him, sweetheart. And he needs you. But I don't want to lose my dog."

She spun on the seat, seeing something in his eyes and face that had her face softening. "You don't? And what makes you think you would?"

"Kade." He looked up as the two men sat. "Afternoon, gentleman. To what do we owe the pleasure?"

Ennis spun back around, her eyes on the men, surprise and then worry and then fear appearing on her face. "Branigan? Brendon? What now?"

"We need to talk to you both. We have new information." Branigan hated to spoil their day but knew the information he had been given could not wait.

"Branigan?" Bradon's gaze shifted between the two. "What do you have?"

"We have received a new threat. Dallas is aware of it and has someone tracing it." Brendon spoke, his voice tight. "This time, it's worse, he says. There is a contract out of you, Bradon. You're to be taken out of the way so this man can get to Ennis. Apparently, he thinks you're the reason he hasn't nabbed her."

Bradon snorted. "As if that were the case. It may be. What else did he say? I know there was more. I can see it in your face."

Branigan sighed. "There was. Your family has been threatened as well, Ennis. We have your parents here and safe. They wanted that. Your brother, on the other hand, we're trying to track him down."

"He's up north." She pulled out her phone as it chimed. "It's Evan. He's safe but says he was met by an RCMP officer and put somewhere safe. This is not how he was to be spending his vacation." "No, it's not how any of you want to live, but at present, you must. When Evan comes back, some of us will head up there and come back with him." Branigan's hand went up at her protest. "Barnabas has talked to him, so he is prepared."

She was on her feet, her eyes on them, before she shook her head and walked away, heading for the elevator. Bradon had risen when she did, watching carefully as she entered the elevator and disappeared before he sat back down. His eyes still focused that way, he spoke.

"What didn't you say?"

Branigan and Brendon exchanged looks. "He's gone past just wanting her, Bradon. He has threatened to kill her once he finds her. How do we do this with you two?"

Chapter 21

Fearing the worst, Bradon was on a hunt two days later. Dallas had called. He was on his way out, and where were the two of them? He had word that Jason had been seen around the building. Bradon's feet took him towards the lake, fear rising in his heart. She hadn't, had she? He knew Ennis was getting restless and wanting to be outdoors, but did she really head for the lakeshore, despite the numerous conversations they had all had with her?

Bradon's feet paused as he heard a voice, his head tilting. He was sure it was the same male voice he had heard before. His feet dug into the sand and he raced towards Ennis, who he could see once more struggling with the man he now knew as Jason. He didn't see the man running towards him until he was tackled and taken down into the cool waters of the lake.

Struggling to get away, hearing Ennis' calls to stop and for help, he just couldn't get free. He felt the man's hand on his head, holding him down below the surface, even as he tried to escape. His vision blurred, and he heard Ennis' calls coming softer and softer until his body just floated in the water, not moving except from the waves washing against him. He didn't see the man wading through the water, then stopping, hands in the air as Bradon's friends ran their way. His assailant was down on the ground and Blair and Benen were into the water, pulling him free of its greedy grasp and carrying him to safety. Depositing him on higher grass, the two men went to work, rushing to save their friend, their glances towards where Ennis now lay still, Baird on his knees beside her.

Ennis had been simply walking, she thought, out for some fresh air when she had stopped, her feet freezing in place, as she looked up to see Jason standing in front of her, a gloating expression on his face.

"Well, well. Who do we have here? Ennis, my dear. And on your own. How convenient." Jason's hand had reached for her, even as she backed away from him, her hands hitting at him to leave her alone. "Not happening, my dear. You're coming with me."

Ennis screamed as she scrambled backwards, her hands hitting at his as he tried to grab her. She heard Bradon's voice and called for him and then for him to get away. He was behind her, she thought, and then heard nothing more from him. She saw the gleeful look that crossed Jason's face before he stopped, his hands rising before one dropped. A knife appeared and she screamed once more, heading running footsteps behind her and her name being called. His hand was back, and the knife thrown before Bradon's friends had reached her.

Braddy had her in his arms and to safety before laying her gently down, a grim look on his face as he saw the knife, sending Brendon and Burnie for the supplies he needed. He knew Branigan had tackled Jason and even now had pulled the man's belt to bind his hands. Branigan's chest heaved as he shoved Jason forward, to stop near Brady.

"Brady?" Branigan's voice was quiet.

Brady shot him a look and shook his head. "We need an ambulance, Branigan. I'm not at all sure she'll make it." He shot a look at Bradon, seeing him on his side, moving slightly as the two men spoke with him. "Bradon?"

"He's good for now. We'll get them there, somehow."

Brady looked up again as Doc dropped to his knees, his hands reaching to help.

"How long?"

"Five minutes, maybe? Ten at the most. I didn't pull the knife." Brady's hands were reaching for the packing material being pulled from packaging for him.

"No, we don't want that." Doc's hands were there, reaching to wrap bandages around the knife and then around Ennis. "We need to keep it as steady as possible." Doc looked around. "We need the backboard and collar."

Burnie reached for the backboard, sliding it to the ground beside her. "We thought you would, Doc. We tried to think of everything you might need."

"Good. Now, gentle as we roll her, Brady. Burnie, at her feet. Buckley, good, you're at her knees." He shot a glance towards Bradon. "Bradon?"

"They tried to drown him, Doc. The guys got to him in time. They're not letting him up until we have help."

Doc nodded, his focus back on Ennis, hearing the sirens coming their way. "Someone go find the men and bring them here. Brady, you ride with Bradon. I'm not leaving Ennis."

Chapter 22

Doc paced the corridor outside the two cubicles, looking up to see Walter walking his way, once more.

"Doc? Someone was knifed?"

"Ennis. It was deliberate from what I understand." Doc sighed as he followed Walter. "And then someone tried to drown Bradon."

Walter paused, his head shooting around to stare at Doc. "What did you just say?"

"I said, Ennis was stabbed. Bradon drowned." Doc nodded at Ennis. "We kept the knife in. Brady was there and took charge."

"That's good. He's got a good head on his shoulders. How long would you say?"

"Thirty minutes at the most. It's not looking good, Walter."

Walter paused and studied Ennis before he reached to pull bandages away, Doc's hands now gloved and helping. "I thought you were done for the day, Doc."

"I was. Thank God I was. With the two of them, Brady was torn as to who to look after. If I had needed him to, he could have taken over Bradon's care."

"This was done on purpose?" Walter winced as he carefully touched the knife. "Deb, we'll need imagining and then call the OR. We'll be taking her there within a short time."

"Already done, Walter. Imaging is expecting you. A CT is what you wanted?"

"Did we do a chest X-ray?"

"We did, as soon as she arrived. Images are up now for you." Deb stepped aside as the team moved into take the stretcher. "How long, ladies?"

"Ten to fifteen minutes." The nurse glanced over at Walter. "Back here or upstairs?"

"Upstairs, I think. Page me when the images are ready." He stared at Ennis as her stretcher moved away and then at Doc. "No, on second thought. I'm coming too. I want to see exacting what is going on."

Doc stood back, his heart breaking for Ennis. He knew her parents were there and were waiting for someone to come and talk to them. He moved across the corridor, to stand watching the activity around Bradon, hearing his rough voice. His head shaking, Doc turned and walked away, his heart heavy, his body slumping, before a hand on his shoulder stopped him. Barnabas and Buckley stood beside him.

"Doc? What's the word?" Barnabas was almost afraid to ask.

"Bradon's talking. I suspect he'll be moved to a room soon. I haven't talked to anyone. That you'll need to do."

"Ennis? Brady said it was bad."

Doc sighed, his eyes on his young friends. "It is. Walter's with her in the CT area. He's taking her to surgery. I just don't know if we'll be able to save her."

Barnabas' face hardened. "But we have him, don't we?"

"We do, I saw. But that doesn't mean he'll stay in jail." Doc's hands ran through his graying hair. "She's not safe, if she even survives."

"Why was she on her own?" Buckley's puzzled question had the two men shaking their heads.

"She's needing to be out. She likely thought she was safe." Doc looked up at Dallas spoke from in front of him. "She was backing away from him, that much we can tell. Bradon must have realized she was missing. We're assuming his are the tracks we see running for the lake." Dallas looked around. "Has anyone spoken to her parents?"

"Not yet. I will." Walter appeared beside him, his finger beckoning for Buckley to follow him.

Walter paused, his eyes on the couple he knew had to be Ennis' parents. "How well do you know them, Buckley?"

"Not well. They've been in our building now for a few days. I've met and talked with them over the last few weeks, since Ennis has been involved with Bradon."

Walter nodded. "That's what I thought. They're believers?"

"They are and strong ones. I just don't know if they're strong enough for what you have to say."

"God will provide that strength, thank goodness." Walter walked towards the couple, Ian on his feet, his face strained and white, Meg's hand tight in his.

"Buckley?" Meg's voice held hope and despair as she spoke.

Walter shook their hands and then sat, after introducing himself. "What have you been told?"

Ian and Meg shared a glance.

"Branigan told us she had been stabbed but not how bad." Ian was desperate to hear his daughter was not as harmed as he envisioned.

"She was. She was stabbed in the chest. I have just viewed the imaging. She's upstairs right now, being prepped for surgery. I'm expecting to be in there for a while." He paused, assessing the couple. "I have to be blunt with you. I can't be anything else. I don't know that she will come through the surgery. At this point, we have not removed the knife. And it is a good thing Doc and Brady made that decision. We would not be having this conversation if they had." He watched with compassion as Ian's arm came around Meg. "Leaving it in helped to stop the blood flow. That we can deal with in the operating room." He looked up as he was paged. "There's my call. Buckley will take you up to the waiting room. I'll send out word as I can."

Chapter 23

His head back against his pillow, Bradon watched through lowered eyelids as Barnabas paced his hospital room, Branigan and Brady leaning against a wall. He had no idea where the rest were, but he assumed somewhere nearby. Dallas had been in, taken his statement and then left before he could ask any questions.

"Barnabas, what aren't you saying? And just where is Ennis?" He waited and then paled at the looks on their faces. "Guys? What about Ennis?" He raised up, pushing at the blankets before he sank back against the pillows. He didn't have the strength to rise. "What aren't you telling me?"

"Bradon, you were almost killed. Don't you understand that?" Barnabas' voice was stern, covering his emotions.

Bradon stared at him, not quite sure. He could vaguely remember coming to, being rolled to his side, and Benen's hand on his side, holding him steady as he coughed and gagged and spewed water. He had heard Blair's voice as well. He couldn't remember seeing Ennis and that scared him. Coming to again in the Emergency Department had not been pleasant, he decided. Still coughing and gagging to some extent, he had barely been aware of his treatment, and then being moved to a room. His glance moved from Barnabas to Branigan and then stopped at Brady. Brady's face was closed, but Bradon knew his friend well enough to know he was extremely upset and worried.

"Brady? What happened to Ennis? I can remember running that way, hearing her screaming, but I don't remember much after that."

"Benen and Blair pulled you from the lake, Bradon. They had to revive you. Do you get that?" Brady's words had a bite to them. At Bradon's nod, he sighed. "Ennis was hurt. That man stabbed her, Bradon. Doc and I worked on her until the paramedics got there."

"How bad?" When none answered, his gaze hardened as it shifted from man to man. "How bad? If you don't tell me, I'll be out of here and searching for her."

Brady walked towards the bed, his hand out to still Bradon's movements, a prayer raising in his heart for his friend's lady. "It's bad, Bradon. We didn't think we'd get her here. Doc stayed with her all the way. His friend, Walter, is the surgeon. Right now, she's in surgery."

Bradon's eyes slid closed. This was what he had feared the most. "She's alive?"

"She is, Bradon. But I talked to Ian and Meg. Walter didn't give them a lot of hope." Barnabas voice was filled with all the emotions he was going through at the moment. "Ian said Walter told them that Doc and Brady wouldn't remove the knife. They left it in. If they had removed it, she wouldn't have made it."

Bradon's eyes were on Brady, seeing the confirmation of Barnabas' statement on his face.

———

"Thank you." Bradon's voice was hushed. "How long?"

"It's been a while. I'm not sure how long she's been in there." Branigan began to pace. "How did he know she'd be there?"

"He's watching that close. Have we searched for any cameras?"

"We're doing that now, Bradon, not that it's any consolation. He seems to have set up somewhere to watch for her. With her going to the beach on her own, that gave him a perfect opportunity. And the man who tried to drown you? That was the police officer Dallas said they were looking for."

Bradon's head shook as he pulled at the plastic identification bracelet on his wrist. "Brady? Find out what you can? Please?" He watched as Brady nodded and then walked away, not knowing what he would find out.

Brady stood for a moment, staring down at his clothes. He had managed to scrub away the blood from his hands and arms, but his clothes were still stained. He looked up as he felt a hand on his shoulder. Breck stood there, compassion on his face, as he handed over a pack.

"Go get changed, Brady. You need to."

Brady sighed. "I do." He hesitated before he looked back up. "We've just told Bradon."

Breck nodded. "I thought so, just by the look on your face. Go. Change. I'll be in the waiting room. Ian and Meg are still in the surgical one. I'm planning on heading that way. They want to speak with you.”

Brady nodded, his eyes dropping to the floor, staring at his stained shoes. “How do we get Bradon through this, Breck? If Ennis doesn’t survive, how do we do this with him? This is worse than it was for the others.”

“It is, Brady.” Breck paused, drawing a deep breath. “I heard from Dallas. Jason ended up in a fight in jail.”

Brady’s head went back. “He’s dead, isn’t he? No justice there. And no end in sight for Ennis. Who was he working for?”

“That’s what I asked. Dallas is clearing off names he’s been given, but still hasn’t come to the one in charge.”

Chapter 24

Their eyes glued to the door to the operating room, Ian and Meg sat, hands clasping one another, just waiting for word. They knew that Anna was around, she had stopped and prayed with them. And the three younger women had been in and out, ensuring they were taken care of. Barnabas had sat with them, prayed with them, walked away to find Buckley to send to them. A nurse had been out not long before, letting them know that Ennis was still alive, that they were working on her but Walter expected it to be a while yet.

"Meg?"

She turned at Ian's voice. "Ian? Have we talked to Evan?"

"I did. Barnabas has sent a couple of his guys up there, to bring him back. He said they were taking the Foundation plane."

"Oh, okay. That's good. He'll want to be here." She sighed as her head went down on his shoulder. "Why Ennis? What did he want from her that badly that he had to try to kill her?"

"I don't know, love. Dallas said they were working on something. Breck said Bradon's friends were as well."

Breck hesitated for a moment before he sat beside Meg, his eyes on her and then Ian. Buckley sat beside Ian, his heart praying for his friend, his lady and her family.

"Breck?" Ian's voice was quiet. "You have word on Bradon?"

"He's awake. Not happy we won't let him up." Breck gave a tight smile. "He was adamant he was coming up here, Branigan said, until he fell asleep."

"That's what he needs. But you have something else weighing you down." Meg studied the younger man.

"I do. Dallas got word to me that Jason has been killed in jail."

"Of course, he would be. That's what would happen. Now, how do we find the others?" Meg's acceptance of Jason's death and its implications stunned the two men until they looked at Ian's face and then nodded.

"Dallas said he was working through what he had and making progress. Just not the kind of progress he wants. He'll need to talk to both of them again at some point." Breck sighed, the day long and not over yet.

"That he will." Ian's eyes rose as he heard footsteps and then he was on his feet, his hand extended to shake Walter's. "Walter?"

"Sit, Ian." Buckley moved so Walter could have his seat, a frown on his face as he watched the looks exchanged between the two men.

"Walter?" Meg's voice was hesitant.

"She's still alive, Meg. God was there, directly every movement we made." His eyes closed for a moment, fatigue hitting at him. "We managed to stop the bleeding. It was as I suspected. If the knife had been removed before, she would have died. We had a time controlling the bleeding. But we did. I stayed with her through Recovery and until we could get her to an ICU bed." He sighed. "This is getting old, you young people getting hurt."

Breck gave a quick grin. "We know that. We've told everyone else this is not to happen. They've just shrugged."

"Can we see her?" Ian reached to wrap an arm around his wife. "We need that."

"I know you do. We're just getting everything settled and set. She's unconscious, as you can imagine, and will be kept that way. Part so she doesn't undo our work. Part for pain control. Suzy will be out shortly to get you. Evan?"

"He's on his way back or will be shortly. Our guys have gone to get him." Breck spoke.

"Good. He needs to be here and Ennis needs him as well." He shared a look with Breck. "How's Bradon?"

"Hurting. He wanted to go find her but fell asleep before he could get up. We'll have a struggle to keep him away from her." Breck walked beside Walter as he moved away towards the exit doors. "What didn't you say, Walter? I know you."

"She still may not make it, Breck. The knife went deep. We've tried to do our best. Only God knows if we've succeeded. Get Bradon up here when you can. They need each other."

"They do, Walter. I have no idea how serious they are, although it was looking that way." Breck sighed. "Only justice won't be done for her. The man was killed tonight in a jail riot, which he instigated from what Dallas said."

"Of course, he would be. But find whoever it is that was behind him. Until you do, she's not safe. And I would hazard a guess that Bradon won't be either."

Breck watched Walter walk away, fatigue weighting his body down before he turned, finding Barnabas standing beside him, holding out a cup of coffee."

"That bad?"

Breck nodded. "From what Walter said, yeah, it was."

Chapter 25

Two days later, Bradon stood, his hands wrapped around the bed rail, his eyes on Ennis as she slept, a drugged sleep, he thought. His heart was raised in praise that she was still alive, but he knew that might change at any moment. Her parents had both spoken with him, and at their request, so had Walter. Bradon understood only too well what the outcome could be.

He studied the monitors, and then shook his head. He couldn't understand them. That's not what he did. When he had returned home the previous evening, Kade had been wild with delight but Bradon could see he was looking for Ennis. He had spoken with Rick, and was to go back to work the next day, working from his office in the building, but he had no real desire to do that, and that concerned him. Where had his drive to work and succeed at doing what he did go?

He felt a hand on his back, and turned slightly, finding Meg there. She had taken him under her wing, she said. He needed her, and she needed him. Evan had been around, compassion on his face as Bradon apologized for not being able to prevent Ennis getting hurt.

"You can't blame yourself, Bradon. She made the decision to go there, on her own. She would have felt she couldn't bother one of you men."

Bradon sighed. "I know. It doesn't make it any easier, you know."

"No, it doesn't. But he would have attacked her then even if one of you had been with her. Look what they did to you."

"They were brutal. I wanted to face him, you know, to ask why." Bradon blinked rapidly, to hide the tears, to keep them from falling, his eyes on Ennis.

"We all wanted that. The other man, the one who attacked you, he's not talking. We think he's afraid of someone."

"He would be. He's a coward."

"He is, but you're not. You have proven that." Bradon turned slightly as he heard Ian speaking from behind him. "Ennis hasn't said, but we can see how she looks at you. You have her heart, Bradon. That much we know."

Bradon nodded, his eyes back on Ennis, his hand resting on her cheek. "And she has mine, but we can't do anything about it. Not yet. It's not fair to her. She has not had the time to be free from that monster, to enjoy life without that hanging over her, and she needs to."

"But if she says no, she doesn't want that? What would you say?" Ian's hand rested on Bradon's shoulder. "Don't let that stop a commitment from you." Ian walked away, his footsteps heavy, not knowing if his daughter would ever get that chance. He had spoken with Walter just moments earlier, unknown to Meg, and the word had not been good. Walter was still concerned that they hadn't been able to stabilize her as much as they should have. He told Ian the knife had missed the heart, had missed the lungs, but had still done damages to the blood vessels.

Meg watched him walk away, praying for him and for her daughter, and for the young man standing with her. She hugged him, leaving him standing beside the bed, his eyes still on Ennis.

"Oh, Ennis, what are we to do? Lord, heal my lady. I'm not ready to let her go. Nor is her family. Lead Dallas and the others to a quick end to the investigation. Ennis can't do this again. It will kill her next time." His head bowed and he didn't even try to control the tears that flowed, not hearing Brady approach, not feeling his hand on his shoulder, but hearing his prayer. He thanked God that he had praying friends. That would help to get them through what they faced.

"Bradon? What's the word today?" Brady spoke quietly, hesitant to ask.

Bradon shrugged. "About what Walter said yesterday. I know he's concerned. He doesn't have to say that."

"No, he doesn't. We've seen too much at times. Barnabas said to tell you that Rick dropped off some paperwork for you. Kade is looking for you as well. He's searching the building and the grounds. We think he's looking for Ennis."

"I think he will be. He's taken with her, sensing her need. And considering she's afraid of dogs, that has to be God that did that."

"God does use our animals, doesn't he? You've seen that many times. I've seen it with patients."

Brady pulled up a chair, shoving Bradon down. "You need to rest, Bradon. They'll be sending you away soon. I'll be in the waiting room when you're ready to go."

Bradon gave an abrupt nod, his eyes on Ennis as she had started to move restlessly, pain on her face. He looked up as the nurse approached, reaching to take Ennis' vitals and then assess her wound.

"Nurse?"

She looked over at him. "You're Bradon?" At his nod, she smiled. "Just checking her over. Making sure everything is fine."

"She's restless. I didn't think she would be."

"It happens. Sometimes before the next dose of medication is due, they can get like that. And yes, she can feel pain, and that can make her restless. Dr. Wilson will be by later." She looked at the clock. "But we do need to ask you to leave."

Bradon stood, nodding, understanding that he did really have to leave, bending to kiss Ennis' cheek before he walked away, away from his lady, uncertainty in his mind as to what he would find when he returned in a few hours. No, he thought. Not until tomorrow. Her family has to have the time with her.

Brady stood, his eyes on Bradon as he walked towards him.

"All set?"

Bradon nodded at the question, turning so he could look behind him

"I am, Brady, but I'm not wanting to leave. Something tells me she's in trouble again."

"She's in good hands here, Bradon. You know that."

"I do, but it doesn't make it any easier." He slanted a glance at Brady. "How much digging have the guys done?"

Brady laughed. "You know us too well. We're digging and digging. Dallas is almost ready to tell us to stop sending him material, but he wants this over for you two. That's what he has said."

"And he's not the only one."

Chapter 26

Ennis could hear her mother's voice, calling her to wake up. She couldn't. Her eyes just would not open. She slipped back to the place she felt safe, knowing that if she did open her eyes, she might not like where she was. Moving restlessly with the pain, Ennis slept once more. It had been a week since her attack, a week of ups and downs. Walter had taken her back to surgery at one point, finding a small area that was still bleeding and repaired it. Since then, her condition had improved.

Meg stood beside her, her hand on her daughter's face, a frown on her own. Ennis just wouldn't awaken properly. They had told her she should be but she wasn't. Meg was afraid, afraid that they could still lose her, that the man behind Jason would appear and Ennis would just disappear.

Dallas had spoken to them, updated them as much as he could with the investigation. She knew it wasn't where he wanted it. Ian said Dallas was waiting for a name or a piece of information that would open up the investigation. She prayed it would be soon.

She turned as she heard footsteps. Bradon and Evan stood there, watching her and then Bradon moved to Ennis' other side. For the first time, Meg noticed that Kade was with him and frowned.

"It's okay, Mom. We talked to Walter. He said to bring Kade in. Maybe that would be what Ennis needed." Evan looked down at Kade. "We know that Kade needs her. I think Bradon has lost a dog."

Bradon just grinned, knowing that wasn't true, but he had decided in the wee small hours of the darkened night that he wouldn't mind losing Kade, if it meant keeping Ennis in his life. Kade tilted his head to look up at Bradon before he stood up at the bed, his nose finding Ennis' hand. Not satisfied with just touching her hand, he leapt for the bed and settled down beside her, his chin on her shoulder, a tongue reaching out to lick at her face.

"Kade, stop. I don't need you licking my face." The hoarse whisper stilled them all and brought their eyes to one another. Ennis had spoken from her sleep.

"Ennis?" Meg bent over her daughter. "Are you waking up?"

"No, I'm sleeping. Is that Kade?" Ennis shifted on the bed, her eyes flickering open and closed.

"It is, dear. Bradon and Evan are here too."

"They are? Where am I? And why does it hurt?"

"You're in the hospital, Ennis." Meg looked around as she heard Walter's voice. "She's awake, Walter, or has been."

Walter nodded, his eyes on Kade. "It took a dog to wake her up? Why didn't we try this before?"

"Because it not likely would have worked, Walter." Bradon reached for Kade, who shifted away from his hand, his eyes still on Ennis. "Kade. Now. Off the bed."

Kade jumped down, his very attitude saying he didn't want to and why would they make him? Bradon watched, a smile lurking on his face, before he looked up at the door. He was away from the bedside, following the man who had been standing there, his phone out to take a photo before the man disappeared. He didn't know him and wondered at the look of hatred on his face directed at Ennis.

Dallas pulled out his phone, sighing at its chiming again. He had not had a break, he didn't think, all day. He studied the photo Bradon had sent, a chill running through him. He knew that man, knew the danger Ennis was in if he had been at her doorway. Dallas ran for Will, had a few moments of conversation with him, before he headed for his desk, his computer programs up. He needed to find this man and find him quickly.Will looked up as Dallas appeared in his doorway, his phone extended towards him.

"Do you know this man?"

Will shook his head. "Not offhand, I would say. Why?"

"Because Bradon just took his picture in the doorway to Ennis' room. The man walked away and disappeared when Bradon approached him."

"That's interesting. Run with it, Dallas, and see what you come up with." Will stared at him for a moment. "You are taking time off, aren't you?"

Dallas nodded. "I'm out of here by six if possible, not working Sunday for sure. But it's a difficult task, balancing the investigations."

"It is. And I know you well enough to know you don't want this to go cold."

"No, I don't." He looked down at his phone and frowned. "Now, Barnabas is calling me." He walked away, phone to his ear, not liking what he was hearing from Barnabas.

Will watched him go and then studied his own desk, rising from it and walking through the department, stopping to speak with the officers and then moving towards the outside, heading for his vehicle. He had to speak with someone and that someone was an hour away.

Bradon had turned back to the room, finding Evan's eyes on him, a question in them that Bradon shook his head at. He walked back towards Ennis, finding her asleep again, Kade huddled down beside her, not looking at his master. Evan gave a snicker at the look on Bradon's face.

"He waited until you turned your back, and then was up there. Ennis was talking to him again before she fell asleep,"

Meg nodded. "That he did. Now, have you heard with the investigation is?"

"Not today, not yet anyway. Dallas did say he was waiting for some information or something." Bradon's arm came around Meg's shoulder. "You've been in here for a while, Meg. Let me take you to the cafeteria and find you something to eat."

Meg looked up at him, wondering why all the men in her life were so tall. She had hoped that when Ennis found her fellow, he wouldn't be quite so tall.

"I can do that. Evan? You're staying?"

"I am. Someone has to. Kade might just kidnap her and disappear somewhere."

Bradon's steps stopped before he spun, a narrowed look on his face before he shook his head. "He just might."

Chapter 27

A week later, Ennis sank down onto the couch in her parents' home. She had needed to be there. Her mother had asked and she did not the heart at that point to say no. Kade stood for a moment before he was up beside her, curling up with his head on her knee. His eyes shifted between her and to where he could hear Bradon. Her hand rested on him even as her eyes closed. She was exhausted, Walter had warned her about that, but she didn't realize just how bad it would be. She contemplated the stairs to the bedrooms and sighed. There was no way she could do them.

Hands on her shoulders shifted her over until the person sat, and then arms wrapped around her, drawing her to him and her head to his shoulder. What was she to do with Bradon, Ennis wondered, and then decided she just didn't know. His actions spoke of his love for her, but he had not said anything. His eyes spoke and she was afraid that hers were answering the question he was asking. Ennis just wasn't sure she was ready for anything else to change in her life. Not at this point.

Bradon watched her, his head tilting so he could see her face, then looking past her at Kade. He just shook his head. Kade was very protective of Ennis, almost too much, Bradon thought, but he didn't have the heart to stop him. Ennis needed someone right now and that someone was Kade. He reached to pull a blanket over her, earning himself a quiet thank you.

"Ennis? How are you doing?"

She gave a small shrug, her head burrowing into his shoulder even more. "I hurt. I'm tired, exhausted. I don't want to be here." She raised her head slightly. "And I have to climb stairs to get to the bedrooms. I just can't do that."

Bradon could hear the trace of tears in her voice, but didn't hear Meg's soft steps that stopped at her words. Meg was away, hunting for Ian or Evan. Ennis would not be climbing the stairs, she thought. There was a full bathroom down here, Ian putting it in for the men's convenience when they came in dirty or muddy. They could set up a bed in Ian's office very easily. Bradon watched her walk away, praying that somehow she had heard and would solve Ennis' difficulties. If she couldn't, he was prepared to wrap Ennis into his arms, take her to Anna, and then stay there himself.

"Bradon? Have they found them yet?"

He shook his head. "Not yet. Dallas wants to talk to us, as does Will. He did say they weren't much further ahead."

"That's what I'm afraid of. That they can't or won't find him and whoever it is appears again."

"I will do everything in my power to make sure that doesn't happen." Bradon had been adamant about that when his friends had spoken to him. He knew they were searching still, but whoever it was seemed to be hiding.

"But I don't want you to be hurt again. That can happen." She yawned, fatigue weighting down her body.

"I know, sweetheart. I know. But I would do it all over again for you."

Bradon wasn't aware that she had cornered the men the day before, finding out exactly what had happened. No one had told her and she just had to know. Horror had flooded her when she heard that Bradon had been drowned but brought back by his two friends. Fear flowed in her that he would be hurt again, and she just couldn't have that. But she couldn't or was that wouldn't make him stay away from her.

"About your dog."

"Kade?'

"Kade. Why won't he leave me alone? I don't like dogs."

"Kade knows you're hurting and need him. He's wired that way. Always has been. He's chosen to make you part of his life. I can't keep him away. He frets and stresses when he can't be near you."

"But he's your dog."

"I know, sweetheart. I know. But dogs are funny creatures. You can own a dog, but the dog will choose who they want. He's done that with you." Bradon bit at his lip before he continued, his voice barely audible. "And he's not the only one."

Ennis shifted until she could look up at him, brushing back at her hair until the blanket was tucked around her once more. "Bradon? What are you saying?"

"That I want you to stay in my life. This is not the time nor how I wanted to tell you. I love you more than anything. I want to explore our friendship, see where we head."

She sighed. "Thank you, Bradon. I was afraid it was all one sided. I love you, too. But I don't want you to be hurt, and that could happen."

"It could happen at any time or in any place. We can't let that stop us, sweetheart." He watched her face closely, seeing when she accepted his words. "So, are we a couple or not?"

Ennis shook her head, her hand clutching at his shirt. "I guess we are. Wake me in an hour." She slept, his arm tight around her, his head on hers, curled up against him, Kade crowding in as close as he could get.

Meg stood for a moment, watching her daughter, seeing content in her face even with the pain and tiredness. They've decided something, haven't they, Lord? They are so suited to one another.

Bradon looked up at Meg. "Meg?"

She shook her head. "Ian and Evan are bringing a bed down for her. We've set up in his office for her for now. She doesn't have the strength to climb up and down the stairs."

"Thank you. I hoped that's what you were doing. I was ready to take her to Anna."

"I know you were." Meg dropped a kiss on the top of his head, just as she would with Evan. "Thank you, Bradon. She trusts you like she doesn't many people. And for her to accept Kade that way? That's a God moment, I would say. She needs you to stay in her life." Her head tilted. "And I think you need her to stay in yours. I know Kade does."

Bradon grinned as Meg finished and then walked away, not telling her that's the conclusion they had come to. Telling them? That would come, at some point. Right now, he was content, holding the woman he loved in his arms, his dog close to him. He pulled out his phone, to scroll through the messages he had received, stopping on the one from Rick, a frown on his face. Who was tracking him to there? He sent a quick reply, asking Rick to contact Dallas or Will, and also Barnabas. This just opened up the investigation a whole lot wider, he thought.

Chapter 28

Shaking his head, Bradon stared at Dallas a couple of days later. He had dropped into the police department, wanting to talk with him about the man who had showed up at his work, and found Dallas deep into their investigation.

"There is no way that person is involved. They're too prominent in that community." Bradon was adamant that the name given was wrong.

"I'm sorry, Bradon, but they are. We're finding out more and more information on them. And it's not good. I can't say for sure they're the ones behind it, but they could easily be. We see it all the time, Bradon. Now, about that man who showed up at your work?"

"That's right. He appeared today. I wasn't scheduled to be there, but I had to talk to Rick about some problems I was seeing with one of our dog recruits." Bradon sat back in his chair, a puzzled look on his face. "I had Rick pull some video and stills for you." He handed over a thumb drive. "They're on there. But that man? I know him from somewhere, and it wasn't good. I just don't know from where."

Dallas listened as he brought up the photos. "Do you know who this is?"

Bradon shook his head. "I have no idea. I was hoping you did."

Dallas sat back, blowing out a breath and drawing in one deeply. "This is Tim Russell. He's a bodyguard for the mayor of our town."

"He is? That's where I've seen him then. But why would he be around, asking all sorts of questions about me?" Bradon shook his head. "I've never spoken to him, barely seen him." His eyes narrowed. "Russell, did you say? We had trouble with someone named Russell a year or so ago. I wonder if they're related." His head went back as he groaned. "He lives in Ennis' town." He glared at Dallas. "Now, you're going to tell me he was involved with that Jason."

Dallas grinned at the look. "We'll not say that. I suspect he was. That means both of you are on their radar." He sat back, his pen tapping on the papers on his desk. "You both have to be so careful right now."

"We know that." Bradon sighed before he stood. "Ennis is hurting so much, part of that being my being hurt because of her. We need this over, Dallas, before she can heal. Both of us want that, I know. Her family is hurting."

"And so are your friends."

"That they are. Let me know what you find out. I'll be heading towards Ennis later today. She wants to move back here."

"She does, does she? Can't stay away from Kade, I gather?" Dallas just grinned at the look thrown him before Bradon disappeared. He sobered at he stared at his computer screen, before reaching to print the photos. He needed to talk to some of the older detectives and he needed to talk to Will.

Will stared at the photos, before looking up at Dallas. "Bradon brought these?"

"He did. I'm heading out to see what I can find out on the streets, but the streets are being very quiet. I know if he tells his friends, they'll be searching as well."

"And you can be sure he will. Be careful, Dallas. If I remember correctly, there are a lot of rumours about this man, and they're not good. I don't know how he's managed to stay working for the mayor."

"Unless the mayor is involved." Dallas and Will stared at each other before Will nodded.

"There are those persistent rumours, Dallas. Run with this. Keep it as quiet as you can for now."

Later that afternoon, Will stood and watched as Bradon and Ennis made their way towards the building and towards himself. He had come out, wanting to see how they were, but also to talk to them. Dallas was on his way as well. They both were concerned enough about the investigation they were ready to find a safe house for the couple, only Will need Bradon would never leave, and that his friends would do their best to keep them safe and alive.

Ennis looked up as she saw him, a smile lighting her face as she stopped, Bradon's hand holding her tight, Kade tight to her other side. "Will? You're here? Good news for us?"

Will smiled as Bradon just shook his head. "How are you feeling now, Ennis?"

"Cooped up. Sore. Wanting to get my life back. Protected. Too much at times." She grinned up at Bradon who was watching her closely. "But you're not here with good news, are you?"

"No, unfortunately, I'm not. Here, let me grab the door. Which suite?"

"Mine, I think, Will." Bradon spoke. "I have more information to give you. The guys have been busy, you know."

"I am sure they have been. I've talked to Barnabas and so has Dallas. Your friends are good."

"That they are." He assisted Ennis to a seat on the couch, shaking his head as Kade jumped up beside her. "Have either of you eaten? I know Anna had set something in the oven for us."

"No, and thank you." Will looked around as Dallas appeared, his briefcase hitting the floor as he reached to help Bradon.

Chapter 29

Ennis watched the three men closely, trying to hide the pain she was feeling. She thought Bradon was picking up on it, but wasn't sure. All she knew was that she wanted this over with, and to go on with her life. Bradon had made it clear he was not walking away, that he wanted her in his life, and she felt the same. Moving her foot slightly, it touched Kade, who was snuggled as close to her chair as he could get. Ennis felt guilty about that.

Bradon pointed to the living room. "We can meet in there, or in my office."

"Let's try your office, Bradon. Is there a couch there that Ennis can lay on? She's about done in." Will reached to support her as she stood, receiving her nod of thanks.

"There is. And I left a blanket there for her."

Dallas watched the young couple before he looked up at Will, who was watching him.

"Dallas? What have you to share?" Bradon got right to the point. "Here. This is for you, and this for you, Will. It's what the guys have come up with. I'm not sure how much you already know."

The two men flipped through the information, Dallas with a frown on his face.

"How did they come up with so much in such a short time?"

"They can concentrate on that only, and I know the ladies have been working when they can. You don't have the resources to do that." Bradon pointed to the paperwork. "They also have sources that won't talk to the police but have provided valuable, at least we think it is, information that may help break this case wide open. We want it over. It's taken too much from Ennis."

Unable to keep her eyes open, Ennis dozed at the men discussed the findings, not hearing Will's exclamation.

"Will?" Bradon waited for him to respond, speaking again when he didn't.

"Bradon, where did Brody find this information?" Dallas had been drawn to a conclusion, the same one he suspected Will had discovered.

Bradon shrugged. "He's the paralegal on the team. I have no idea where that came from, but he did say for you to call him. He expects that."

"And I will. He has picked up on something we may have overlooked, or not found yet in the investigation." Dallas finally sat back, his eyes straying to Ennis. "She's asleep."

"She is. She crashes early since her injury." Bradon reached to wake her, stopping as Dallas shook his head.

"It's okay, Bradon. We just wanted to touch base with you two, to see how you're doing, to see if you had any other thoughts or idea. We'll need to work through what you've given us."

The men spoke for a while before Will and Dallas left, leaving Bradon to clean his kitchen, and then head back to the office, a cup of tea for Ennis and his own cup of coffee in his hands. He sighed as he watched her sleep. He needed to wake her but it hurt his heart to do that.

Ennis roused, sitting up to take the cup of tea with a quiet thanks. She looked around through blurry eyes.

"Will and Dallas? Where are they?"

"They've left. You slept through them talking to me."

"I did? What did they have to say?"

"First, let me tell you there was a man who appeared today at my work. They've identified him at Tim Russell."

"Russell? As in bodyguard Russell? As in muscle for hire?"

Bradon's head tilted as he studied her face, watching as she pushed her hair away from it.

"That would be him. Do you know him?"

"Everyone in my town knows him. He's always been known for that. Doesn't he work for the mayor here? Or is it is wife he works for?" Ennis looked up, a thought hovering in her mind. "Did you know Jason is related to her?"

"He is? Did we overlook that?" His phone was out as he sent a quick text off to Branigan. "I'll let Branigan look into that. They may have discovered that." He stared at the text message he had just received. "Branigan says they found that out and passed it along in the documentation to Dallas and Will. I didn't know the man until today. I don't know how they came up with that, but they had some reason for finding it."

"Your friends are good." She stared at him for a moment, before looking down at Kade. "I'm sorry, Bradon."

"You're sorry? For what?" Bradon was puzzled.

"For involving you in this. You shouldn't have been. And I'm sorry Kade is sticking so close to me. He shouldn't when he's your dog."

Bradon just grinned at her. "Kade is doing what he's been trained, in part, to do. He works with me during the day. In his off time, he's spending time with a friend. And if he spends time with this friend, then I get to as well." He paused, gathering his thoughts, which became dark as he thought of what she had been through. "I'm not sorry I got involved. I wouldn't have met my lady if I hadn't."

"Do you really mean that, Bradon? You're just not saying that to appease me? Make me accept Kade when you know how scared I am of dogs?" She was desperate to know exactly how he felt, but wouldn't come right out and ask him.

"I mean every word and more. You are my love, sweetheart, the one I've been waiting for. Let's find these people who are after you, and then we can decide where we want to go."

"That's not fair to you. It may take ages to find them." Ennis rose and walked away from him.

Before he could rise to his feet, he heard the click of the outside door and knew she had left. His head went back on his chair as his eyes closed and his heart hurt for his lady, praying that she would find peace somehow in all this, and that this would be over soon. That was his feeling, Bradon decided. That it wouldn't go on for long, not with Russell tracking him down as he did.

He looked down as his phone chimed. Rick? What now? He read the text message and groaned. No going into the building for him then, he decided, not if there were cars and people moving around there the security feed had captured. Rick would bring him the work he needed to do, the text read. And then Rick asked how he was, how Ennis was, and what could he do for them?

Chapter 30

A week later, Ennis was on a hunt, once more. Only this time, she didn't quite know what or who she was looking for. She had driven herself back to her hometown, sending Bradon a text message that she was there. Ennis wandered the downtown area, greeting friends, before she finally entered a shop. An antique shop she decided would be just the place to hide contraband. She didn't think it was all about her. Now, Jason might well have been involved in things she didn't want to even imagine, and she prayed she was wrong, that ladies and girls hadn't really disappeared under his drive to money, but she could see that. He had stalked her for so many years, and she had run from him. That hurt, she decided, that she had lost time with her family and friends that she would never get back.

Ennis searched the store, finally focusing on the old books, which she handled with care. A lump rose in her throat as she picked up one. This was what she was looking for, and didn't know. She walked quickly to the cash desk, paid for the book, and walked away, her eyes searching for anyone watching her.

She almost ran for her car, sliding into it, and locking the doors, her eyes on her purchase. There had to be an answer here, she thought, but how do I find out? Her phone chiming startled her, and she glanced down at it, her breath coming in sharp gasps.

"Ennis? Where are you?" Bradon's voice came through and she could hear the worry.

"I'm at home. I'm heading back your way. Can you stay on the phone with me, if I leave it on speaker?" She was worried, more worried than she had been in years. She thought she could feel someone watching her but looking around, she didn't really see someone.

Bradon was waiting in the parking lot for her, pacing, worried more than he wanted to show. Breck paused on his way through and then detoured to talk to him.

"Bradon?"

"Breck? Don't you have a meeting or something?"

"I do. Just wanted to make sure you were okay. You seem to be pacing."

Bradon grinned. "Is that what this is called?" He sobered. "Ennis went back to her hometown this morning. She's on her way back. We were on a call, but the call dropped."

"And you don't know if she's safe or not." Breck nodded, turning as he heard a vehicle. "I would say she is."

Bradon spun, then almost ran for her car, stopping short as he watched Ennis through the window. She looked out at him and he drew in a deep breath at the raw fear he saw. Wrenching open her door, he reached for her even as her seatbelt released.

"Ennis?"

"Bradon? He followed me. I am not sure who he is, but I managed to grab a photo of him and his vehicle." She clung to him, and he could feel the shudders running through her.

"That's good. Here, let me have your phone. I'll pass it one." He glanced up at Breck, who was nodding, before he walked away. Bradon knew that the search would commence, even though Breck had a commitment he had to be at.

"Wait, Bradon. I found this." Ennis reached for the book and then her purse. "This was in an antique store in town. I think it might have some information we need."

"That's good." Bradon took the book, and then wrapping an arm around her, led her to the building. "You didn't want company this morning?"

She shook her head. "I wasn't really sure what I was looking for. But when I saw the old books, a memory triggered. Jason had said something one time about that book. I just ignored it and shoved that memory away."

"You've remembered now." Bradon swung her around to walk towards the building. "Do you know what is so important about it?"

She shook her head. "Not really." She stared down at his, her eyes puzzled, before she groaned. "It's a family history, Bradon. About the Russells. Was Jason related?"

"I can't remember, but we will figure it out. That I can guarantee you." He held the door for her, and then followed her in, his eyes meeting Blair as he walked towards them. "Here's Blair. I know Devaney's home today. How be we go see them?"

"We can't just drop in on them. That's just not acceptable." She was horrified at the thought.

Bradon grinned at her. "It's okay, sweetheart. Blair's right here."

"He is? Where did he come from? I didn't know he was here." She looked at Blair and then down at the book, suddenly thrusting it at him, almost dropping it in her haste to be rid of it. "Here, you take it. I don't like it. I don't want it anymore."

"If you don't like it, why do you have it?" Blair was puzzled, even as his smile still lit his face.

"I have no idea. I saw it and just knew you needed it. Will it help?"

Blair glanced through it. "It might. You took a chance bringing this back, didn't you."

Bradon nodded. "She was followed. I sent a photo and license plate over to Breck and also Dallas." He paused, his eye on Ennis. "Is Devaney at home?"

"She is. In fact, she had sent me to find you two. To see if you would like to join us for lunch?"

"Food? Did you say food?" Ennis was almost running for the stairs. "I didn't eat this morning. I'm starved."

Bradon stared after her, remembering to snap his mouth closed. "Did she just do that? And she's not supposed to be running."

Blair was laughing at his friend. "She did, and no, she isn't. I think the idea of food was uppermost in her mind, not her safety." He paused, sobering. "How is she really doing, Bradon? We can't get a reading on her."

Bradon shrugged. "I have the same trouble. She's learned to hide a lot of what she's feeling and thinking. Her Mom says that's not her. She should be very vocal."

Blair stared to laugh once more. "You will have your hands full, my friend. Let's find our ladies before Ennis eats our portion of the lunch."

Chapter 31

Devaney watched Ennis closely, see how tight to the edge she was and then shook her head. Ennis was getting ready to run and when she did, Devaney feared she would never return, and either take Bradon with her or leave him behind, devastated.

Blair sat as well, his eyes assessing Bradon before turning to Ennis. He nodded to himself. It was coming to a conclusion, soon, he thought, but how did he and Bradon's friends force that. He finally rose, returning to the table with the book, and sat back down near Ennis. Ennis shuddered as she saw the book, not sure why. She felt Bradon's arm come around her and leaned back against him.

"Blair? We need to pray first, I think." Bradon spoke, his eyes on her. "Ennis needs that."

"You both do." Blair stared at his friend before he did just what Bradon had asked, for the couple and then for their friends and then the police officers work on their case.

Ennis looked up with the men had finished, thankful she had praying friends. She studied the book and then poked at it, afraid of what they would or would not find when it was opened.

"Ennis?" Blair's laughing voice brought her head up. "Would you like to open it?"

She glared at him even as she shook her head. She was exhausted to her very bones, she thought, and wanted this over. Bradon needed to get on with his life, and then she could too. She really didn't believe that he meant what he said. Bradon's arms tightened on her, letting her know through his touch that he cared. She leaned back on him before she spoke.

"We do need to open that. I don't know why I was led to it. I've never seen it before."

"And you are afraid people will think you planted it." Devaney's soft voice broke through the silence that ensued after Ennis' words.

"I am. That's exactly what I am afraid of." Ennis looked up at her friend. "How did you ever do it, Devaney?"

"With a lot of prayer. Support from our friends. Support for and from each other. It was the same for Baird and Berneen and for Benen and Cadee." She suddenly grinned, startling them. "I already feel like I have a laundry list of friends this has happened to. Do you think it will affect each one of you?"

Blair just shook his head at his wife, even as Bradon laughed, and then answered her. "With the rate we're going, more than likely. I mean, after all, how are they to find their ladies, unless they come to their rescue in the ladies' distress?"

Ennis stared at him for a moment before a small smile lit her face. "Thank you, Blair. Now. This book."

"This book. I understand you had someone following you today."

"I did. Bradon said he sent the picture to Breck and also to Dallas." She shifted until she could turn her face to him, to find him watching her with his head tilted to see her face. "Bradon? You did, didn't you?"

"I did. Breck had it before he left for his meeting. Dallas let me know he had it and had someone working on a name. He'll let us know as soon as he can."

Ennis nodded, reaching for the book, hesitating as she did so, a sudden fear running through her. She clenched and then unclenched her hands, knowing she needed to open the book, but not wanting to.

"Ennis? Do you want me to open it for you?" Bradon's voice was soft in her ear, his breath blowing at her hair.

She shook her head, blinking rapidly. "No, I think I need to. I'm just afraid of what I'll find, of what I'll open up. Does that make sense?"

"Perfect sense." Devaney's voice was equally quiet. "If you can't today, you could leave it for another day."

Ennis shook her head. "No, I need to do it today. God help me, please. I just don't know."

She slowly opened the cover on the hardback book, a frown on her face. "This is a diary, I think." She looked up at Bradon, whose hand rested on hers.

"It is, Ennis. That's what it is, I think. A diary. But why would it be the store? Shouldn't family members have it?"

"That's what I don't understand." She looked around.

"What do you need?" Bradon watched her closely before glancing up to see Blair shaking his head.

"My phone. Did I give it to you?"

"You did. I never got it back to you." Bradon handed it over. "Why?"

"Because I need to call Mom or Dad. Ask them about the Russells. They know them, not well, but they will have an insight we might need." Ennis sat back, her eyes on the book. "I'm sorry, Blair, Devaney. This will take a lot of time and you two have commitments in the morning."

"Actually, we don't. It's Saturday." Devaney shook her head at her friend. "You've been through so much. Our actual worry is that this will be too much for you,"

Ennis stared at her and then at Bradon. "We need this over for Bradon. He should never have been involved." She turned her attention to her phone, not seeing the brief look of sorrow and another emotion his friends couldn't read that crept across his face.

Chapter 32

The next morning, Ennis stopped short in the doorway to the boardroom, snapping her mouth closed. All the men are here, she thought, already at work. She saw the three younger ladies around a table to the side and noted the coffee, tea, and food on that. They've prepared for a long haul, haven't they, Lord. Her eyes raised to the walls and she frowned.

Bradon was watching her closely, seeing the emotions that were fluttering across her face, and saw the exact moment she caught on to what his friends were doing.

"Just like in the movies, Ennis, only we have to use paper and our boardroom walls."

"They've been busy. This can't be just from this morning."

Barnabas shook his head as he came to a stop in front of her, his eyes doing his own assessment of her. Doc had asked that of him. "No, they've been working for the last week or so on this. They have made some progress, and that information has been sent on to Dallas. He was quite impressed with how they worked on it for Blair and Devaney."

"So, we're not the first?" Ennis made a move to the side, to study the whole room, before she felt Bradon's arms around her.

"We're not. We've told you that. And no, I pray that we don't go through everyone else." He laughed at the look on Barnabas' face. "It was commented on last night that we still have a number of friends for this to go through." He gave a quick look behind him and then moved Ennis to the side so Dallas could enter.

"Your guys are just too good, Barnabas. How do they discover this stuff?" Dallas, a grin on his face, held up a thick folder.

"Probably because they don't think like you do." Ennis' comment caught them by surprise. She didn't see the startled looked throw at her.

"What do you mean, Ennis?" Dallas was curious, never having had that comment made to him before.

"You think like the police. They think like ordinary people trying to solve a puzzle." She looked up, a spark of mischief playing across her face. "And this is what it is, a huge puzzle that I want solved." She moved away from the men, leaving them staring after her.

"She's right, you know. Now, how do we solve this puzzle?" Bradon moved away, intent on finding out what was happening and what more information had been discovered.

Barnabas snickered at the look on Dallas' face. "Can we do that? Solve this?"

Dallas shook his head, an answering grin on his face. "I hope we can. At least, I mean, I pray we can."

Barnabas' hand on his arm kept him from moving forward. "Dallas? Care to explain?"

Dallas shook his head. "It's you. It's your friends. Their ladies. Doc and Anna. Will. Even going through what Blair and Devaney did and now what Bradon and Ennis are facing, and seeing their faith not wavering, I had to search. Even though Bradon was technically dead and Ennis so close at times, I had to search. Someone kept them alive."

"And that Someone is God, is that what you're saying?" Barnabas' eyes raised to Will, who stood behind Dallas, a surprised look on his face, that changed to happiness.

"I guess I am. I just wonder why I never did that before."

"Because you weren't ready for it. God has used my two friends, and when you tell them that, they will be overjoyed."

Dallas shook his head. "Surely, He could have used an easier method."

"Not all the time. Besides, they went through what they did and are at present to bring someone to justice."

"And there's that." Dallas walked away, towards Burnie who was beckoning to him.

"Did you suspect that, Will?" Barnabas' voice was low.

"I wondered. He has changed, become more settled. I talked to his girlfriend. Katie's a believer, knew she shouldn't be dating him, but did. She is overjoyed that he is now a believer."

"That's good. Now, about this."

"Yes, about this. Dallas showed me the photo Ennis managed to snag. Do you know who that is?"

Barnabas shook his head. "No. I haven't seen it." He took Will's phone, staring down at the photo. "It's not, is it?"

Will nodded. "It is. He's related to Jason, to the Russells, our good mayor's wife. How far does it go?"

"I fear for my friends, Will. These people are brutal and will stop at nothing." Barnabas walked away himself, heading for Doc, who stood watching closely.

Will shook his own head and headed for Ennis. He needed to talk to her, to see how she was. He saw the fatigue in her face, the paleness of it, the stress that had caused fine lines. He turned to find Bradon beside him.

"She's not sleeping?"

Bradon shrugged. "She won't say. Kade doesn't want to leave her side if he's around her. I've never seen him like that."

"But then he's never seen you interested in a lady."

Bradon grinned. "And there's that. Where do we really stand, Will?"

"Dallas knows better than I do. He's planning on updating you two and I gather all your friends today. He has found some interesting tidbits, as he calls them." Will studied each man before he spoke again. "This is where it gets very dangerous, Bradon.

Your friends will need to take care, as will the ladies. Dallas was able to identify the man in the photo.”

“And that, I take it, is not good.”

“No, it’s not. It opens up a whole new line of investigations.”

Chapter 33

Dallas stood beside Burnie, his head tilted as he listened to him. Burnie was an author, and as such, had been handed the diary for the first look-through. He had scanned it quickly and then sat back, worry in his mind for his friends. This was not just an ordinary diary, he thought. Looking around, he had caught Dallas' eye and beckoned him over.

"Burnie? What do you have? It's not good, that much I can tell." Dallas perched on the side of the table, a foot swinging idly.

"Not, it's not, Dallas. How did she ever get ahold of it?"

Dallas shrugged. "From what Bradon said, she was in her hometown, went into an antiques store and was looking around. She felt drawn to the books and found that." He stabbed a finger at it. "What can you tell me? Or can you already?"

Burnie nodded. "It's not just a diary. It's actual a step-by-step history of the Russells, and how deep they were into crime. How did they ever let it go?"

"We'll ask them that. How much can you tell me already?"

"Not a lot, not until I go through it more thoroughly. But it is frightening. It names Ennis' parents."

Dallas sat upright more. "It does. But why?"

"That's what I'll need to dig through." Burnie took a better look at the book. "It's not really that old, I would say, and not that thick. How be I make a copy, let you have the original for your team to go over, and I'll work from the copy. That way, I can mark it up all I want."

"That sounds like a plan." Dallas looked around. "Do you have to leave here to do that?"

Burnie grinned. "Not at all. Barnabas has the rooms all stocked with whatever equipment we need, and that includes a photocopier. I'll be right back." He was on his feet and away to the other side of the room, Ennis' eyes watching him before she turned back to Buckley.

"How do we pray for you, Ennis?" Buckley pulled out a chair beside her and sat, his eyes watchful, catching Bradon moving around on the edge of his line of sight.

"I don't know, Buckley." She sat back, her brow furrowing as she thought. "I guess. I don't know. I guess, safety for my family, for Bradon, for all of you. For all of this to be over. That way Bradon can go on with his life."

Buckley nodded. "But that's not quite what I wanted to hear."

"It's not? What did you think you would hear? Pleas for me?" She shook her head. "I don't do that, Buckley. I don't ask prayer for myself."

"And in this case, you should. You need it." Buckley prayed hard as he watched her. "How be we pray like this? We pray for what you've asked for. But we also pray for you, as Ennis, as an individual."

"And what would you pray for?"

"I would pray like this. For your peace. For your safety. For wisdom. For strength. For courage. For your family. For your friends. For Bradon."

She watched him closely as he paused. "We need to pray for you. You bear a heavy burden at any time. But now? You are bearing much more of one."

Buckley smiled at her. "You understand, don't you? This is when I remember that we were prayed for in the Garden. And that all we need to do is touch the Master's garment. Just the very edge of a hem, and we can be healed."

"That has gotten me through so much." Ennis looked around, her eyes narrowing on Burnie. "How is Burnie making out with the diary? I know he was handed it."

"I have no idea. Shall we go over there and ask him?" Buckley grinned at her as his eyes raised to Bradon standing behind her. "Maybe Bradon knows."

"Bradon doesn't know. Burnie has not said, although he has passed the original on to Dallas, Ennis. He kept copies of it. That way, he says he can mark them up." Bradon paused, biting at his lip. "Dallas would like to speak with you."

"But do I want to speak with him?" Ennis sighed as she rose, heading for the door, and away from Dallas. "You talk to him. Any questions he has? Write them down and get them to me. Right now? I'm crashing and need to sleep."

Ennis was out of the door before Bradon could stop her, a nod coming from Brennen as he followed her.

"Ennis?" Brennen voice stopped her in her tracks. "Are you okay?"

He watched as her shoulders shook with sobs, before he walked up and just hugged her. "Do I need to get Bradon for you?" He felt her head shaking.

"No, I don't want him hurt again, and I am just so afraid that's what will happen." She pushed away from him. "How do I get him to stay away from me?"

"That won't happen, Ennis. I can tell you that. No matter what or who you face, he will be there or he'll find a way to get to you. That's a given. We can all see how he feels about you." His voice compassionate, he continued. "And I would say that's how you feel about him." He wrapped an arm around her and steered her for the lobby and then to one of the couches, pushing her down and sitting on the coffee table in front of her. "So, tell me. Let me ask once again. What do we do for you?"

She shrugged, her eyes on the floor, hiding or so she thought her emotions. "I don't know. I have asked my family to stay away, and God help me, I need them. I can't have them near me."

"We get that and so do they. But they'll be here if you need them. That's a guarantee. But what do we do for you?"

She shrugged, startled as a cup appeared in her vision as Cadee handed her a cup of tea. Brennen took his mug of coffee with thanks. Cadee moved to step away when Ennis caught her hand.

"Please? Cadee? Stay? Brennen was just asking what you all can do for me."

"Other than the obvious?" At Ennis' nod, Cadee settled back on the couch, a leg tucked up under her, her own cup balanced on her leg. "That's a tough one, Ennis. We all know what we want for you, what Bradon likely wants, what your parents and your brother want. I saw Buckley talking to you and I have a pretty good idea of what kind of pep talk he handed you. He's good at reading people." She considered what she should say. "For you? I would say, first we need to end this. But before that, we need to get you well." Ennis stared at her, dumbfounded at how she narrowed in on that.

"How did you know?" Ennis' voice was barely above a whisper, fatigue washing through her as did relief that someone understood.

"Because to a certain extent, we've been there. We've never told you our story but when Benen and I were running for the aircraft, I was shot with a small dart. That dart was poisoned. I almost died that night, just like you, and if Benen hadn't mentioned that I said I thought I had been stung by a bug, it would have been overlooked."

Ennis' eyes were huge as Cadee finished. "That happened to you?"

"It did and much more. Some day, I'll tell you the rest of our story. Some of it is down right ugly. Now, you and Bradon. Do you know what happened to him that day?" Cadee felt led to share what had gone on that day.

"No, and I wish someone would tell me. All Bradon does is shrug it off, says it's in the past, and that he's more concerned about me."

"It is all that, but more, Ennis." Cadee reached for Ennis' cup, setting it past her on the table by the couch. "If you don't put that down, you'll spill it. Apparently, Bradon went looking for you, heard you yelling, tried to get to you and was tackled. He was held down in the lake." Cadee watched with compassion as Ennis' face whitened.

"He wasn't, was he?" Ennis felt the tears in the back of her throat and swallowed hard, her eyes focusing on the turning leaves on the trees surrounding the building. "He wasn't hurt that bad, was he?" When neither one of her companions responded, she turned back. "Cadee? Brennen?"

"For all intents and purposes, Ennis, Bradon died that day. He was drowned. Blair was one of the ones who reached him quickly and worked on him." Brennen knew he would never forget his friends racing for the water and then lifting his eyes to what they were running for and that he never would forget the sight of Bradon's lifeless body being carried from the water, seeing him laid on his back, and the two friends working frantically to clear his lungs and bring him back. He remembered the relief that had surged through him when Bradon finally started coughing and hacking, being rolled to his side to help with that.

Chapter 34

Her hand covering her mouth, Ennis stared at Brennen in horror. She had not known that what was had happened to Bradon. He had brushed it off, not wanting to talk about it, more concerned about her.

"Brennen?" Her voice was barely audible. "Is that what happened?"

Brennen nodded, his eyes on her, sorrow in them. "It is, Ennis. He never wanted you to know. He refused to tell you and didn't want us to, either. But you needed to know. He almost lost his life coming to save you. That's how much he loves you."

Cadee's arms were around Ennis in a hard hug. "That is so true, Ennis. We almost lost you too, then."

Ennis nodded. "I know. Walter talked to me. I made him. Mom and Dad didn't want me to know how bad it was, not right away. But it's my body. I needed to know that." She sank back, reaching for her cup to take a sip. "But where do we go from now? I mean, with the investigation. Dallas talked to me last night."

"He did? And?" Brennen leaned forward, his arms resting on his thighs. "What did he say?"

"That I was right. That Jason was related to the Russells, on his mother's side, I think he said. And they found evidence that he won't talk about, that showed Jason had been stalking me for years. We're just not sure why. Dallas said he had an idea, but he had more work and thought to put into it before he would talk with me. I don't like that, but I have accepted it." She looked up as she felt hands shifting her over and then someone sitting beside her, arms wrapping around her pulling her back against a body.

Bradon had been standing out of her line of sight as Brennen had spoken. He had shaken his head. He had never wanted her to know that, at least not yet. He didn't want her turning to him out of gratitude, them making a commitment to one another, and then Ennis walking away from him. He could not handle that, he thought.

Ennis shifted enough she could look up at him, a frown on her face. "Bradon?"

"I'm okay, sweetheart. I'm okay. It happened. And I would do it all over again to save you." He watched as she sat, a puzzled look on her face.

"Who did it?"

"What do you mean?"

"Who held you down like that?"

"The one who had been with the police. I'm not sure how much you remember."

"Not a lot. I can remember walking out towards the lake. I needed some freedom, some space. I had told security where I was heading, but I gather they didn't get to tell you?" She watched as Bradon shook his head. She sighed. "Somehow, he found me. I don't know how. He threatened me, tried to drag me away. I can remember screaming and fighting and seeing the other man run away. Then, I don't remember anything."

Bradon nodded before his chin rested on the top of her head. "That's how we cope. God provides us the needed ability to forget some things. This is one of those times, sweetheart."

"But, Bradon, you didn't tell me about you." She was dismayed but also angry to a point that he had hidden something from her.

"No, I didn't. I wanted you to heal more first, but you did need to know. I didn't want to tell you though."

"It involved me. Don't ever hide anything from me again."

"I won't." Bradon shared a look with Brennen. "That's a promise. Now, about the investigation."

"What about it?" She was disgruntled and it came through loud and clear.

"Dallas has had to leave. You didn't see him go?"

"I did. He waved on the way by. He'll be in touch. That much I know." She twisted to look up at him. "What did your friends come up with?"

"A lot, actually. They've been working on it off and on since you were first hurt. They upped their time working on it."

"They shouldn't. They have their own lives to live."

Brennen shook his head, catching her attention. "It's what we do, Ennis. We work together as a team, two teams actually. I don't think it has ever been explained to you that we're divided into two teams, along the lines of what we do. Barnabas would need to explain his reasonings to you. He's the one best to do that. But we do step outside of what we do and how we volunteer when we need to. And this time, it's for you and Bradon. Not one of our begrudges the time we've had to take. We realize it could be one of us. Three of us have already gone through it. So, don't apologize. And don't run. If Bradon's not around and you need someone to help you, each one has said that."

She finally nodded, finally getting it that she had become part of that family Bradon belonged to, a family drawn together by choice and not blood. She knew she had a lot yet to overcome, Jason had seen to that. She shifted how she was sitting, drawing up her legs, her head going down on Bradon's shoulder as she slept, feeling safe, secure, and loved.

Brennen watched her closely, nodding as Cadee rose and gathered their mugs, her comment softly spoken that she had an errand to run. Bradon's eyes were on Ennis, his love for her not shuttered for a moment.

"Bradon? What did Dallas really say?"

Bradon gave a soft sigh as he looked up. "He's afraid it's going cold. Any lead they have that looks promising dies out. If he doesn't get something soon, he'll have to put our investigation to the side."

"That's what we're afraid of. Ennis can't continue to live like this. Nor can you."

Bradon shrugged. "It is what it is. We'll deal with whatever happens." He looked down as Ennis stirred, her eyes opening slowly as she looked around, finally focusing on him.

"Bradon? Is it over yet?"

"Not yet. We're working on it, sweetheart."

"Oh, okay. I dreamt it was all over. I was so hoping it was." Her head snuggled down on his shoulder again, before she looked up, lifting her face enough to kiss his cheek, stilling his motions. "Wake me when it is, please? I love you." The two men stared at each other, wonder on Bradon's face, mirth on Brennen's at the look on Bradon's. "Marry me?"

Bradon stared down at her for a moment, then kissed the top of her head. "In a heartbeat, sweetheart."

"Okay. Today, then?" Ennis was asleep again before Bradon could respond.

Chapter 35

An hour later, Ennis sat upright on the couch, shock and disbelief on her face, as she shook her head. Bradon and Brennen had talked, had prayed, and then Brennen had left, to return with fresh mugs of coffee for them and a bottle of juice for Ennis.

"I did no such thing!" Ennis was adamant that she had not asked Bradon to marry her.

"But, you did. Brennen heard you. And you asked to have the wedding today."

"No, I didn't!" She stared at him as he continued to shake his head, before she turned to appeal to Brennen. "Tell me I didn't, Brennen."

"Sorry, Ennis. You did. You took Bradon aback, I think. He wasn't expecting that." Brennen was having great difficulty containing his mirth.

Her head back, Ennis groaned. "And I can't take it back, can I?"

Bradon was laughing himself at this point. "No, you can't. And I accept. So, I guess we're engaged." He laughed harder at the glare she shot him. "It's okay, Ennis. I'll let you off the hook, if that's what you want."

Brennen shook his head at the two, seeing the concern lurking in Bradon's eyes before he glanced at Ennis. His head tilted as he studied her, seeing something on her face that didn't go with their conversation at present.

"Ennis?" When she didn't respond, Brennen spoke again, raising his voice just slightly.

Ennis jumped, then stared at Brennen. "Brennen?"

"Ennis? Where were you just now? You weren't here in the lobby with us."

"No, I wasn't. I was…." Her voice died away. "I'm not sure. I can remember seeing Jason heading my way and I ran and hid. He searched for me. Now, where was it?" She shifted in Bradon's arm, her hands clutching at his. "I can see him so clearly. See the hatred and malice on his face. Why did he hate me? That's what I don't get."

"I would say it's because you kept escaping him and then ran, staying as far away from him as you could. You kept your family safe by doing so." Breck sat down into another chair, drawing all their eyes to him as he spoke.

"Is that why? I always wondered. I thought it was me."

"In a sense, it was. He wanted you, for reasons that Dallas and his team are just uncovering. No, I'll let him tell you. All he said was that it wasn't pretty, and he was glad the man was dead. But we still have to watch you carefully, until we find the ones behind him."

"He wasn't working on his own?" Ennis spoke quietly, a frown on her face. "How do the Russells fit in them? He's related to them. I spoke with Mom and she confirmed that."

"Dallas has managed to get that. What else has your mother indicated?" Breck was searching for any little thing that could solve this mystery.

"She didn't say much." Ennis stared at Breck. "I just wish I had lived in another town."

"That didn't happen. Now, what did you just remember?" Breck grinned at her.

"I'm not sure if it's something I actually remember that happened or have been told." She paused, her hands rubbing together. "It's Tim Russell. Did you know there are three? Tim, Tom and Tam. They all look a lot alike. I think it was Tam that hung around with Jason. They were close to an age. Jason was about five years older than me. What did they do?"

Breck shook his head. "I didn't know that. I'm not sure that Dallas has made that connection." Breck has his phone out and was sending a text off to Dallas. He stared down at his phone before he looked up at Ennis. "He didn't have that connection. How do you do this?"

"Do what? Make the connections? It's called living in a small town all my life." She sighed as she leaned back. "What else can I tell you? The rumours were there that the three lived life on the edge of right and wrong. Tom actually is in prison right now, convicted of manslaughter in a drug deal gone wrong. Tim is working for the mayor here, but I doubt he got that on his own. He was known to do a little blackmailing." She sighed. "The mayor's wife? Connected to the Russells. We were all surprised that he got in as mayor, given her history."

———

"That bad?" At her nod, Brennen shared a look with the other two men. "That gives us a new line to trace. And I think one of the guys already had that thought."

"You're ahead of me, then. Thank you for that. I wish I had more information."

"We've talked to your parents, to Evan, to others in your town. There is a lot of fear out there, but what happened to you? And to Bradon? That has changed how the people feel about them. They are tired of living in fear, of not being free to go about their lives. They wanted us to thank you."

Ennis nodded once more, watching as Breck stood and excused himself. She studied Brennen,

"Don't you have to be somewhere?"

Brennen and Bradon grinned at her even as Brennen shook his head.

"Not right at the moment. I'm waiting to hear the wedding plans."

Ennis groaned and buried her head against Bradon. "I'll never live that down, now will I?"

Bradon just hugged her tighter, his mirth-filled eyes on Brennen, before they raised past him, and his arms tightened on Ennis, even as Brennen caught his look and moved to rise, his body flying forward to lie on the floor, sent there by the vicious blow to the back of his head.

Chapter 36

Ennis screamed, her scream echoing through the lobby, even as Bradon rose and pulled her with him away from the men. He stopped suddenly as he felt the gun barrel poking him in the back, not letting go of Ennis. She shook, fear for Bradon coursing through her, even as she glanced down at Brennen.

Please, Lord, let him be alive. Get Bradon out of here somehow. I don't care about me. She screamed again as she was torn from Bradon's arms, a hard grip on her wrist pulling her away from him. She struggled to escape, managing to do that, hearing Bradon's shout for her to run. She ran, her feet slipping on the hardwood floor, before she was tackled and taken to the same floor. She struggled once more, a flying hand catching her assailant in the face and releasing her. She scrambled to her feet, running from the area until a hard blow to her knee sent her facedown to the floor, her hand reaching for the area, sobs of fear and pain forced from her.

Ennis didn't hear the struggle that Bradon was putting up, seeking to release himself, and get to her. She didn't see him forced from the building and into a waiting vehicle, the doors slamming behind him, and then the vehicle racing away.

The men who had been in the boardroom looked up, startled, as they heard Ennis scream and then, on their feet, ran for the door, wrenching it open and racing towards the lobby. Brady and Doc were on their knees beside Ennis, even as some of the others ran for the outside. Brady was on his feet, moving towards Brennen as Blair called for him.

"What happened here?" Barnabas stood, staring between the two, and then looking around. "Where's Bradon?"

Doc shot him a glance. "Ennis said men appeared, knocked Brennen down, and then Bradon told her to run. She doesn't know what hit her or where he is."

Burnie's sudden yell from the security desk had Barnabas heading that way. He stared down at the security guard, and then up at the destroyed equipment.

"They did a number on that stuff, Barnabas. Mick's alive but he needs help."

"I can see that." Barnabas sighed as he pulled out his phone. "We just can't catch a break, can we?" He walked back towards Brennen, finding him sitting up, as Brady looked him over. "Brady, Mick needs you. He's down."

Brady shot him a glance and then nodded. "Brennen seems to be fine, but we'll know more once he's assessed. Any word on Bradon?"

Buckley spoke. "It seems they took him with them. No sign of him around. We can see scuff marks on the sidewalk where it looks as if he was struggling to get away." He looked around. "How did they do it?"

"They took out Mick, and the security equipment at the same time. I would suspect Bradon or Brennen saw them coming and tried to intervene."

"I would say Bradon. Brennen was sitting with his back to the hallways when I walked by thirty minutes ago." Buckley rubbed at his face, his eyes going to Ennis. "How is she?"

Doc had approached, leaving Ennis in the care of Benen and Baird for a moment, as he looked towards Benen. "Her knee is damaged. How, I'm not sure? She's in too much pain to think clearly. Why did this have to happen? Hasn't she had enough? And I have no idea how bad it is."

"I know, Doc. We all know that." Breck spoke from beside him, his hand on the older man's shoulder. "Ride with her when they go. Brady's gone to assess Mick."

"Mick?" Doc spun, held in place by Breck's hand.

"They knocked him out, surprised him, I would think." Breck's hand dropped from Doc's shoulder as he moved towards the security desk.

"Okay, Barnabas. Who goes with who?" Breck looked around at the gathering men, the ladies watching from near the elevators, their arms around one another.

"Brady with Mick. Doc with Ennis. Some of you can head in. The rest, I want working on this. Call your employers. For now, you're here, in this building, or out searching. We meet for prayer at seven in the morning and again at seven in the evening." He turned, searching. "Buckley, tomorrow's Sunday, but get the prayer chain working."

Buckley nodded and was away to the other side of the lobby, watching as the emergency vehicles approached. He sighed to himself. No one needed this right now, did they, Lord? But You are in control. We just need to remember that. Keep our friend, Bradon, safe, and heal both Ennis and Mick and Brennen. This is hurting our guys, Lord. This isn't the first time one of them have been taken from this very land, but not from inside the building itself. These people are getting bolder and bolder all the time.

Chapter 37

Later that day, Meg stood at her daughter's bedside, once more, watching as Ennis moved restlessly. She knew Ian and Evan were around. They had been in with her but left to find Barnabas or Breck or Dallas or even Will. They wanted to know exactly what had happened to Ennis. And just where was Bradon? She had been looking for him to find Ennis, but he had not appeared.

Meg turned as she heard the door, to find Ian walking towards her, a stern, shuttered look on his face.

"Ian?" When he didn't answer, she reached to grip his arm, even as his eyes studied his daughter and then the equipment surrounding her.

"Meg? How is she?"

"Lucky. There was some damage. Doc explained it as tears to the cartilage and tendons. They're waiting to do surgery, wanting to see how the knee repairs itself." She shot a glance back at the door before turning Ian to face her. "Ian? What's going on? How did this happen? And where's Bradon?"

"Bradon? They're not sure." Ian's hand reached out to touch his daughter's, stilling her movement.

"What do you mean? They're not sure? Isn't he here?" Meg spun to stare at the door.

"No, he's not. He's disappeared. At the time Ennis was hurt."

"And just how was she hurt? I can't get anyone to tell me."

"She was running from some men who appeared in the building lobby. I guess she and Bradon and Brennen were talking. Brennen was knocked out, Bradon yelled for her to run. She had a bit of a scuffle with her attacker and in trying to get away was hurt. Bradon seems to have been kidnapped."

"Kidnapped?" Meg's voice rose as she said the word, her mouth clamping closed as she finished. "Brennen? Is he okay?"

"He has a headache and is very angry. Somehow, the men who appeared took down Mick, the security person on duty today, destroyed the equipment, and then made their escape." He looked back down at Ennis, before turning to Meg, sweeping her into a hug, feeling the sobs shaking her body, a prayer rising within him, a prayers without words that he knew would be heard.

Evan stood for a moment, watching his parents, his heart hurting for them. He walked quietly to stand at the foot of the bed, watching Ennis, seeing her eyes flickering before he moved up beside her.

"Evan?" His mother's voice brought his head around and he reached to hug her.

"Mom? What's the word?"

"No surgery as yet. They're waiting to see how it does. Surgery is a possibility, but she'll not be bearing weight on that foot for months." Meg watched Evan closely, seeing a small smile he couldn't hide. "Evan?"

"They didn't tell you?"

"Who didn't tell us what?" Meg shared a look with Ian, worry in her heart.

"Apparently, Ennis asked Bradon to marry her. And today. But then, again, she was almost asleep when she did that."

"She didn't, did she?" Her mother was dismayed. "Not another one of her almost asleep requests. We should have warned Bradon."

Evan just shook his head. "Apparently, he agreed. These two are in love, Mom. I just don't know how much they know that, or where they're heading."

Ian sighed, having had a heart to heart talk with Bradon. "Bradon loves her, he's told me that, but he won't go any further with it until this is over, and she's had a chance to live as a free woman, he said. He seems to think she needs some time just to be her, without something hanging over her head."

"And that she does."

Ennis roused as she heard her family, her eyes finally staying open, groaning as she moved. "Mom? Dad? Evan? Where am I?"

"You've been hurt, Ennis. You're in the hospital." Meg's hand rested on her daughter's head.

"I am? What did I do? Never mind. I don't want to know." She slept again, leaving her brother with a grin on his face, that changed to a frown as he saw Dallas and Barnabas approaching through the opened door.

"Barnabas? Dallas?" Ian turned, watching them closely. "You're here. Something is up."

"Yes, there is." Dallas paused, assessing them and then Ennis. "How is she?"

"She was awake briefly, but is out again." Ian studied them. "You're not here for just that."

Dallas sighed, his eyes meeting Barnabas. "No, we're not. We have to put all of you under protection now. Barnabas has suggested his building." Dallas' hand went up. "We know. It was breached today, but for the foreseeable future, all doors will be locked, and he has brought in more security. That team is hurting, not just because one of their men was hurt, but because Ennis and Brennen were as well and because Bradon disappeared."

Ian nodded. "It makes sense, but Evan and I still have to work. We can't just walk away from that."

"We know. We're making arrangements to transport you both back and forth. In fact, one of the teams will take you back, Ian, to your place, and Evan to yours to gather some belongings for you all." He nodded at Ennis. "Doc has agreed that she should be in the infirmary there. It will work. He's taking a leave from here for now and Anna is a retired nurse. We'll make do."

"We need to do more than that, Dallas. This is twice Ennis has been hurt this bad. And Bradon? Is he still alive even?"

"He will be, Ian." Barnabas spoke up. "They want him alive to get to her. They took him with that thought in mind, more than likely. We'll receive a ransom note, of sorts, directed at her, that will want to make an exchange."

"Exchange?" Ian was puzzled for a moment. "You mean, Bradon for Ennis?"

"That is exactly what I mean." Dallas stared at the floor for a moment, before he looked up, a bleak look on his face. "I can't tell you how sorry I am this happened. I was out there this morning, talking to them all, finding out what information they had I could use. Will was there. Whoever it has been, had to have been watching. We have officers searching the area right now."

"You won't find him out there." Evan walked over to stand in front of Dallas. "I have an idea."

"You do? Care to share?"

Evan shot a look back at his sister. "Sure. Just not in here. I don't want Ennis to wake up and hear us."

Dallas nodded, even as he followed Evan out of the room, listening closely as Evan spoke, shaking his head at times, before he turned and walked away, walking back rapidly, his hand out to pull Evan with him, beckoning to Breck and Brady as they watched the two men.

Chapter 38

His head spinning from the blows he had taken, Bradon lost his balance, his hands and knees hitting the floor of the room he had been shoved into. He had stayed like that for a few moments, his head hanging down, trying to get his balance back, before he raised his head and then sat back on his heels. He looked around, surprised at the cleanliness and tidiness of the room.

Rising to his feet, Bradon searched the room, not finding anything he could use to protect himself, but also finding the door to the hall locked. He paced, opening the doors, finding a huge walk-in closet and then an ensuite. He stopped there to reach for a cloth he wrung out under warm water and swiped across his face.

He turned from there to feel along the windows, staring out them at the well manicured lawns, the tidy buildings around the yard, the neat driveway that wound through the area. Where was he?

Bradon refused to turn as he heard the door open and then the sounds of a tray being set down. He peeked at his watch, surprised to see how late it had gotten to be. They must have driven him around for ages, but for how long, he wasn't sure. He turned to contemplate the door and then walked over to study the tray. Supper, he decided, lifting the cover off the plate, surprise at the meal set there. He sighed, before he reached for a chair. Bradon decided he needed to eat, needed to keep his strength up.

Bradon finally rose, walking back to stare out the window again, seeing the sun setting, throwing out the pink and purple and red shafts of light. He finally drew the drapes and turned to the bed, sitting on the side of it before laying down, and pulling the blankets over him. His eyes closed, as he prayed. He had no idea where Ennis was, how she was. He had heard her scream and then sobs of pain before the men had wrestled him out of the door and into the vehicle, where he was shoved to the floor and a blanket thrown over him. Bradon worried about Brennen, not sure how hurt he had been.

He was puzzled. How did the men get into the lobby? They should not have make it past Mick. Then, he sighed, knowing that Mick must have been hurt. He prayed for his friends, but also for his lady, a slight smile cracking through the grimness on his face as he remembered her request and then her denial. Ennis, we really do need to talk, don't we, sweetheart?

Bradon slept, not hearing the door open or the tray removed after the man had entered on silent feet and stood over him, nodding that the sedative in the food had worked. He hadn't liked that when he was told it had been done. He knew the man lying in front of him. Bradon. He worked for Barnabas, he knew. The man's gaze lifted as he stared in front of him and then glanced back at the door before looking down at Bradon. He had heard bits and pieces of the conversation around him, being ignored as he usually was. Somehow, he had to get Bradon out of there and he would.

A week passed like this for Bradon, alone in the room, only seeing the man's shadow as he brought in and then removed the trays of food. He felt sleepy all the time, almost groggy, not realizing he was being sedated. Bradon wondered when he would be asked the questions he thought he should be, or be taken out and killed. That he knew was a real possibility. He prayed for his love, for her family, for his friends. He didn't really care about himself anymore. He didn't think he would be walking away alive.

His hands on the window frame, Bradon stood one afternoon, once more watching the dusk coming in, swaying as he stood, unsteady on his feet. He turned to head for the bed, knowing he needed to lie down, but his eyes closed and he slipped to the floor, not hearing the thud his body made, not feeling as his head hit hard on the rug overlaying the hardwood floor.

The man dropped the tray to the table and hurried to Bradon's side, his hands feeling for a pulse. He sat back on his heels, his eyes on Bradon, before he turned to the open door. He was alone that late afternoon. Now was the time to make his escape and take Bradon with him. He had nothing of his own that he really cared about. What little he did care about, he carried in his pocket. He pulled Bradon to his feet, and over his shoulder, heading for the stairs and the outside. Unlocking his vehicle, he gently set Bradon on the seat, securing the seatbelt before he rushed to slide into the driver's seat, carefully searching for anyone watching. He would head out the back way, he thought. That was how the hired people always came and went. They would not be able to track him, at least, he didn't think so.

They were not there to hear the curses and blame when the owner of the house found the empty room, the forgotten tray sitting on the table by the door. The man spun, orders flying from his mouth along with the spittle of his rage. The employees or hirelings or whatever you wanted to call them ran to do his bidding. Some ran, just to escape. They had had enough. The talk among those few was that he was mad, that he would hurt Ennis even more that she had been. They hadn't liked the fact they were now accessories to kidnapping. They had all agreed that they would find some way to escape his clutches and make their way to the authorities. Now seemed to be the right time to do that.

The birds and night creatures gradually crept forth from their hiding spaces, filling the night with their sound, covering the thundering footsteps and curses from inside the house. He was on his own for the moment and rage filled him. She would pay, he declared, and so would he.

Chapter 39

Ennis shifted on the couch she was sitting on. She was back in her suite at the building, Doc having moved her to the infirmary for a few days before he let her move home. She knew Anna was around somewhere. Ennis had told Anna she could manage, that her Mom would help, but Anna had just given her a look and continued to take care of her. She was grateful, she thought, but she felt like she was putting so many of her friends at risk.

Ian had talked with her, had told her what had happened as far as they could determine. She had watched him, nodded, said it was about what she had expected, and then thumped away on her crutches, leaving her father staring after her, not sure if she really understand what risk she was still at, or if she even cared.

Evan had approached her that morning, sitting with her, not saying anything. Ennis appreciated that about her brother, that he could be quiet with her when she needed that.

He had finally turned to her, a twinkle in his eye. "Did you really ask Bradon that?"

Her brow furrowed as she tried to remember. "Ask him what? Evan, what are you talking about?"

"Brennen said you were almost asleep and then suddenly just asked Bradon to marry you. When he agreed, you asked it be that day." Evan was openly grinning at his sister by this point.

"I did no such thing!" She stared at her brother, horrified at what he was saying. "Evan! I didn't do that!"

Evan kept grinning at her even as he shook his head. "But, you see, you did. Brennen heard you. And Bradon agreed."

Ennis' head went back as she stared at the ceiling, before her eyes slid shut. "I did it again, didn't I? Almost asleep and making a request. How many times have I done that over the years?"

Evan simply shook his head. "I have no idea. Usually it's something simple or something easy for us to get for you. This is a tough one, you know."

Ennis nodded. "I know. I have no idea what I was thinking."

"That you love him and that you know he loves you. You are a couple, whether you agree or not, sis." Evan sat forward, his eyes on his clasped hands. "Did you really mean that?"

"Mean what?" Ennis watched her brother. "Oh! That! Asking him to marry me?" She shrugged. "I guess. I usually do when I make those requests. I haven't done that in a long time."

"No, you haven't. In fact, I don't think you've done that since before you moved away. It's usually when you are under stress that this happens. Ennis, what aren't you telling us?" Evan twisted his neck so he could watch his sister. "What is it, sis? There has to be something."

Ennis sighed. "I think there is. Did you see that old briefcase I used to use in high school?"

"I did." Evan was on his feet, moving quickly to where she had set up her office, and then was back, the briefcase in his hands to give to her. He watched as she sat, her own hands resting on its soft sides. "Ennis? What is it? Come on, tell me. You used to tell me a lot, but not everything. I would have stopped this monster."

"I know. That's why I didn't tell you. He would have killed you or had his friends do that." She studied her brother. "I couldn't let them do that to you."

"I wish you had told me." He watched her closely for a moment, before he nodded at the briefcase. "What's in there?"

"I can't rightly remember. I think....I don't know." She reached to open it, stopping as Evan's hands covered her, not seeing Branigan and Baird coming in and sitting silently near her, or Dallas stepping in behind. Barnabas had stopped in the kitchen to have a word with Ian.

"We need to pray first, sis. Let's pray. I fear for you and what you have in there." Evan watched as her face whitened and then hardened into resolve.

"Please, Evan. Please pray that this is over and Bradon is back with his friends, unharmed."

She jumped as she heard the other men take up the prayer, followed by her father. She hadn't realized so many had gathered around her. She had felt her mother's arm around her as Evan had prayed. Ennis looked up, tears sparkling in her eyes as they finished, a silent thank you on her lips.

Ennis stared down once more at the briefcase before she spoke. "Dallas? Any word?"

"No, I'm sorry, Ennis. We have a lead we tracking but nothing yet. I wish I did have news for you."

She simply nodded as she reached to unbuckle the briefcase, pausing before she folded back the flap, and then she opened the briefcase, staring inside, pausing once more before she continued to reach her hand inside, pulling out the papers inside before her hand felt around inside. She pulled out the small packet that had hidden itself in the lining, a frown on her face, before it clear.

Ennis looked up at Barnabas. "I'm sorry, Barnabas. I'm so sorry."

He frowned. "Why are you apologizing, Ennis?"

She held up the packet. "I had this. I had forgotten about it. It is proof, I think, of what Jason had been involved in. I think it also lists people he worked with. I'm sorry. If I had remembered, then maybe Bradon wouldn't have been hurt."

"I don't think it would have mattered, Ennis." Dallas spoke up. "There is just so much we are uncovering about him. All I can say is I am thankful God kept you out of his hands."

Ennis nodded. "I know only too well what he intended. He told me, many times. I had forgotten some of it, burying it deep inside me. I never wanted Mom and Dad to know. And Evan?" She turned to her brother, tears on her cheeks. "He would have killed you if you had gone after him."

"You told me that, sis. And I have no doubt he would have tried." Evan reached to grip her hand, finding hers ice cold. "What is in that packet?"

She turned it over and over and then handed it to him. "Here. You can open it." She gathered up the papers and turned to Branigan. "Here, you take these. Copy them for Dallas. I tried to document everything I knew, every time he approached me, every time I got a card or a letter or a photo."

Branigan studied her carefully before he looked down at the sheaf of papers, covered in her tidy handwriting. "All this?"

She nodded. "All that. Maybe, there is something in there." She sat back, Meg's arm around her, even as they heard a noise at the door, Barnabas rising to answer it, a surprised tone to his voice that brought the men to their feet.

Chapter 40

Barnabas reached out a hand, gripping Bradon's upper arm in his hand, even as he stared past him at the man standing there. He frowned, thinking that he knew the man, before Dallas was there beside him. The man was ushered in, hesitation in his manner, even as Barnabas led Bradon to the living room, finding Ennis' eyes on Bradon, shock on her face.

Ennis stood, her eyes on Bradon as he wavered in the living room door way, her brother's arm helping her to balance. Somehow, Bradon found her, gathering her close, before Evan shoved them both down onto the couch. Bradon landed heavily, taking Ennis with him, not hearing her muffled groan of pain as the movement jarred her knee. Evan watched with sympathy before he helped her to shift her body to a more comfortable position, her legs up on the couch, a pillow tucked under her injured one.

Quiet conversation surrounded them before Dallas sat near them, his mouth open to speak, snapping it closed. He turned to Barnabas, catching the look on his face before he settled back. Ennis had her head turned, watching Bradon, seeing how difficult a time he had been through, just by his face.

Dallas finally spoke, after studying Bradon, watching as he took the mug of coffee with thanks. Ennis frowned, her eyes tracking between Bradon, Dallas, and the man who had returned Bradon to her. She caught the man's slight shake of his head before she sighed to herself. Okay, now what, Lord, she thought. Obviously, something is going on here I don't know or understand. But You do.

His eyes on Ennis, Barnabas spoke. "Bradon? Talk to us. Tell us what happened."

Bradon just shook his head, his eyes heavy. "I really don't know, Barnabas. All I can remember is trying to get back to Ennis before I was dragged outside and shoved down into a vehicle. A blanket covered me. They drove around for ages, I suspect, because when I was shoved into a room, it was late afternoon or early evening." He paused, gathering his thoughts, fatigue making his thought processes difficult to understand. "They never took me from that room, never asked for anything. Absolutely nothing. I got my meals, but the supper meal must have been drugged. I barely remember finishing those meals before I collapsed and slept." His eyes raised to the man who had freed him. "Thank you. You don't seem to fit with them."

The man shook his head. "I don't. I was put there for a reason, God only knows that it must have been for you. I don't know much about what they were up to. I was only the low man in the group. They talked some around me, but not a whole lot. I never saw the owner of the house, but I would say he's someone with money."

Bradon nodded, then wondered why he had done that, the headache spreading behind his eyes. "I think you're right. The room I was in was decorated tastefully, shall we say?" His head went down on Ennis' and he slept, not hearing Doc approach, or hear the men moving away.

Meg gently tucked a blanket over Bradon, waiting as Ennis moved to sit up, Bradon's arm tightening around her. Ennis turned her head to study him, seeing his face relaxing as he slept, knowing he was free once more.

"Mom?"

"He's not letting you go, is he, dear?" Meg's voice held amusement. "You two need to come to an understanding." She turned as she heard a snicker from Evan.

Ennis tried to hold back her groan. "I think we already did, Mom. I just didn't know it." She glared at her brother. "Evan, shut up."

Meg stared at Evan, and then turned back to Ennis, seeing her daughter burying her head in her hands. A trace of humour showed in her voice as she spoke.

"Ennis? What did you do?" She waited, not hearing Ennis speak, but hearing the snickers from Evan. "Ennis? You didn't?"

Ennis nodded, her eyes on Bradon. "Apparently, I did, Mom, and don't remember. Apparently, he said yes."

"Oh, Ennis! Not another of your requests when you're almost asleep?"

"It was, Mom." She turned back to her mother. "And I wanted to marry him that day, from what I'm told."

"Ennis, my dear!" Meg sat on the coffee table, reaching for her daughter's hands. "You have not done that in years. It only comes out when you

are really stressed." Her head bowed and she prayed
for her daughter.

Chapter 41

Shaking his head, Ian pointed to the outside door, beckoning Dallas and Barnabas with him, nodding at Doc as he passed them to enter the apartment. He stood, a hand rubbing at his face, his thoughts on his daughter's words and then Meg's.

"Is that true?" Dallas' voice held a bit of awe at Ennis' admission.

Ian nodded. "More than likely. Evan talked to me. Apparently, she asked Bradon to marry her, when he said yes, asked that it be that day. She doesn't remember doing that." He sighed, his arms crossing over his chest. "She has a history of doing that, of asking things just as she's almost asleep. Although, it's always been small things and things we can easily accommodate for her. This, this is something new."

"Stress will have done it. Bradon makes her feel safe, I would gather." Barnabas shook his head, a small grin on his face. "Brennen had mentioned it to me."

"He did? I didn't realize he had heard." Ian was surprised.

"He was there. Now, where do we go, Dallas?"

Dallas had been listening to the two men, but his attention had been directed at the apartment door. "First, I take Bradon's rescuer down town and have a talk with him. Bradon's in no condition right now to give more of a statement than he has." He looked up as the door opened and Doc appeared.

"Doc?" Barnabas' voice was quiet but they could hear the concern in it.

"He's still sleeping. He likely will for a while. From what the man said, the cook always put a drug in his supper. Bradon may not have realized what was happening, or else he didn't care."

"Probably both, Doc. I don't think he expected to come home." Barnabas turned and walked away, deep in thought, heading for the boardroom and the men gathered there. They needed to find these people and fast, he thought. It will not go well for Bradon just to have disappeared. And how did they keep his presence quiet? He sighed at that, knowing Bradon would not be agreeable to just that plan.

The men were scattered through the room, deep in their work, all looking up as Barnabas entered, closing the door behind him, and just standing, his eyes on the floor.

"Barnabas?" Burnie spoke for them, their eyes meeting in puzzlement. "What's going on?"

Barnabas looked up. "Bradon's home. One of his captors just walked in with him." He waited as the men reacted, sounds of surprise and joy in the room, before he continued. "Thing is, he was sedated, we think, the whole time. He doesn't remember a lot."

"And now we need to hide him? Is that what you're saying?" Brandon spoke up.

"He'll never go for that." This from Brennen. "Where is he?"

"Right now, he's sound asleep on Ennis' couch."

"And not letting go of her, I suspect?" Brennen grinned. "Do we have a wedding to arrange?"

Barnabas' grin cracked through the grimness on his face. "I have no idea. It's up to them to tell us. Right now, we just need to solve this. Where do we stand? Dallas has taken Bradon's rescuer down town to talk to."

"How did he get here?" Brady spoke from where he stood at the printer.

"His rescuer said he just walked out with him and drove away. They were the only ones at the house at that particular time."

"God!" Buckley's smile lit up his face.

"That's it, Buckley. God brought him back. Now, God will lead us to the answers." Burnie buried himself back into the notes from the diary, wanting to finish that day. He had found a trace of something, and had pulled Ennis' notes she had handed Branigan to compare.

Breck walked over to stand beside Barnabas, his shoulder against the wall, watching the men as they once more buried themselves into their work.

"How is he really, Barnabas? What kind of help will we need to find for him?"

Barnabas shrugged, his eyes on the floor, deep in thought. "Right now, Doc has looked him over.

He'll do a better assessment when he's awake. Dallas will be back around, and I'm sure Will may make it out at some point. I would like to see him talk to someone, but I doubt he'll remember a lot. For now, he's where he needs to be, with Ennis."

"And how is Ennis?"

Barnabas shook his head. "I have no idea. Did you know she had a habit of making requests like that? Apparently she hasn't in a while, and nothing that major."

Breck stared at him for a moment before he smiled. "And this is a major one. I can see Bradon teasing her about that for years to come."

"So can I. The thing of it is? I don't know if they'll stay together." Barnabas sighed. "Didn't we just go through this with Blair and Devaney?"

"We did, but theirs was totally different from this." Breck turned to the door. "I'll head up there, and then talk to security to see what we need to do." He stopped, his hand on the doorknob. "And I can tell you this. Neither one will want to be hidden away. They'll be out there, on their own if necessary, to draw out the culprits."

"That's what I'm afraid of, Breck. That they will do just that."

Chapter 42

Staring at Ian, Bradon finally just shook his head. He could not just marry Ennis, even though she had asked him, and he had agreed. He turned his head to stare towards the living room before he walked across the kitchen, his socked feet quiet on the floor, and reached for the coffee pot, to stand hands resting against the counter, not quite sure what he wanted.

Ian watched with compassion as Bradon moved in almost slow motion before he reached out a hand, tugging him from the kitchen, and hand on his back, directing to the bathroom.

"Get cleaned up, Bradon. I know you'll welcome a shower. Breck was through your place and brought some clean clothes for you. For some reason, he didn't think you would want to leave my daughter's side." He had a grin on his face that reminded Bradon of Evan.

Bradon shook his head. "A shower and clean clothes sound good. There was a shower where I was but I refused to use it. I guess I was stupid not to." He swayed for a moment, grabbing ahold of the door to keep his balance.

"No, I don't expect you did." Ian watched Bradon closely. "Are we needing to have a chat, Bradon?"

Bradon turned carefully, his eyes on the older man, before he sighed and nodded. "I guess we do. I love Ennis more than I thought I could love anyone." He grinned suddenly, the sternness and fatigue disappearing. "I guess you heard what she asked of me."

Ian gave a low laugh. "I did. Evan has kept it quiet, but I am sure the men all know. They won't tell a soul, I know that much. She'll be teased but it will be without malice." He paused, his eyes on the floor for a moment, before he raised them to study Bradon. "Go. Get cleaned up. I'll make you some breakfast and then you'll need to sleep again. Ennis finally headed to bed early this morning. We had to make her leave you."

"You did?" Bradon shook his head. "Thank you, Ian. You have raised a fine daughter who is caring and compassionate. I want this over for her and for you." He closed the door, standing with hands on the vanity, staring at his image in the mirror. Lord, I know what I want. But it's what You want that matters. Help us to help her overcome what she's faced for years.

Bradon finally pushed away his plate, thanking Ian for the food, before he cradled his mug in his hands. He felt somewhat more awake but was still groggy to some extent. Whatever they had given him over the past week was still affecting him. He knew from Ian that Dallas planned to stop by that morning, as early as he could, to get his statement. He also knew from Breck that the men were still hard at work, pulling information from the copy of Jason's diary and from the notes Ennis had handed them. It would take time, but he was reassured that they were making progress, and that progress was being passed on to

Dallas, who just stood and stared at them whenever they handed him something new.

Ian stood for a moment as he heard movement from down the hall, watching as Ennis headed his way, her crutches thumping along the floor as she did. His heart was saddened for his girl, knowing that the injury may curtail what she loved best, to bike, to run, or just go for a long walk. He had talked with Doc in general and that talk had not gone the way he would have liked.

"Dad?" Ennis paused for a moment. "You're here?"

"Your Mom and I have been all night. She's gone home to get some sleep. I'll do that when she's back." He tilted his head to watch the emotions playing across her face. His next words were quiet enough that only she could hear him. "Ennis? What are you thinking?"

She shrugged. "I have no idea, Dad, other than being thankful Bradon is back, angry that he was taken, angry that I'm hurt, and anxious about what is happening." She gave a small smile. "Is that enough?"

Ian shook his head. "It is for now." He pointed at the kitchen. "Bradon's up, had a shower, and has eaten. We've talked, the two of us. He loves you, you do know that?"

Ennis nodded. "I do, Dad. I thought I had ruined it asking what I did."

Her father grinned at her. "Not at all. He just wishes it had been him doing the asking, but he wasn't sure enough of you to do that. He's still learning how to read you."

"Is that what you call it?" Balancing the crutches against her, she reached to hug her father. "And what decision did the two of you make for me?"

"None. It's your decision, Ennis. Yours and Bradon's." He gave a low laugh. "I hear tell the fellows are thinking an early wedding."

Ennis shook her head. "Not with this hanging over us, Dad. And Bradon wants me to have some time where I can enjoy life like that, to experience life as a young woman says. At least, that's what he has said to me."

"And he's right. You're overcoming this. I can see that. God is blessing you with many new friends, all of whom want to help you." He stepped back, pointing to the kitchen. "Go on. Find your fellow. He's waiting for you."

Bradon stood as she entered, his eyes searching her face, before he just swept her close to him. They finally sat, quiet conversation between them, not talking of what had happened, talking instead of what their hopes and dreams had been as youths and what they were now. Their talk drifted to different scripture verses they loved, surprised to find they shared so many.

Dallas stopped to watch them before he approached the table, his portfolio going down on the wooden table top. He reached to pour himself a cup of coffee before he sat, his eyes studying the two, finding them watching him.

"Dallas?" Bradon finally spoke.

———

"Bradon? We'll need to get your statement today. Now, if possible. Then, we'll need to talk."

Bradon shrugged. "Okay." He watched as Ennis stood, reached for her crutches, and walked away.

"Did she just do that?" He asked of Dallas.

"She did. She needed to. She can't be here when you give your statement." Dallas reached to open his laptop, setting up a video camera, and then nodding at Bradon. "Whenever you're ready, we'll start."

Chapter 43

Dallas finally sat back, his eyes thoughtful, before he reached to print Bradon's statement, handing it to him with instructions to read it over, make any changes, initial them and then sign it. He waited, seeing the fatigue weighing Bradon down and then rose, heading to find Ennis.

She was standing, balancing on her crutches, as she stared out the living room window. She turned, her eyes going past Dallas to the kitchen, before she looked at him.

"Dallas?"

"He's done. Just proofreading it for me." Dallas' head tilted as he studied Ennis. "How are you, Ennis?"

She shrugged. "I have no idea. Everyone keeps asking me that."

"And they will. They're concerned." He hesitated, then spoke. "I need to talk with you both. Can you come back to the kitchen, or no." He pointed to the couch. "Sit. Doc tells me that you need to elevate that leg as much as possible." He watched as she seated herself, helping to settle the pillow under her knee. "Now, Bradon and I will be right back."

Bradon appeared in the doorway, before he headed for Ennis, shifting her enough that he could sit beside her, then reaching to hand her the mug of tea he had made. Dallas returned with his notes and his own refreshed cup of coffee before he sat, his eyes down, a prayer in his heart.

"Okay, Dallas?" Ennis' voice was soft, hesitant, not like hers at all. "Where do we stand? I know you and your fellow detectives have been busy with our case as well as many others. Will has stressed that. And I know Bradon's friends have been busy as well."

"That we have, Ennis. That we have." His eyes found hers, a look in his that she could not read. "I can only say how sorry I am you had to face him on your own."

She shrugged. "It's in the past. He can't hurt me anymore. But his friends and whoever it is that was behind him can."

"Talk to me, Ennis. I know there are things that you have not said to anyone."

Staring at him, Ennis finally nodded. "There are. He was a brutal, vindictive, sadistic man. No one knows what he threatened me with. How he threatened my family. How he threatened to harm anyone if I sought help." Her face had whitened at the memories.

"Why don't you just talk, Ennis? I'll make notes. Then, when you're ready, we'll discuss them. I don't think you'll say anything that will surprise me." His eyes lifted to watch Bradon, whose own eyes were on Ennis. "Now, do you want Bradon to leave?"

Ennis' face turned to Bradon, seeing in his eyes his love for her, his acceptance of what she might say, his trust and confidence in her, and shook her head. "No, he can stay. This is just so hard."

Bradon's voice broke through the silence that ensued, raising a prayer for strength and courage for his lady, wisdom for Dallas, and an end to it all finally for her.

Ennis' hands tightened on Bradon's. "It's hard, you know. I've buried it so deep, that it hurts to bring it out. But I know I need to. And the hurt will heal, but I'll never be the one I was before this all started.

"It started, I guess, when I was around sixteen, seventeen. I didn't know he was watching me until he approached me one day. I ran from him, but he kept coming after me. I tried to make sure I was never alone, but he somehow managed that at times. The things he would tell me? No teenage girl should ever hear them." She paused, shudders of horror wracking her body, the almost silent tick of the grandfather clock the only thing breaking the silence.

"He tried to get me to do drugs. When that didn't work, he tried alcohol. I refused, telling him to leave me alone. I told him I was going to my parents and to the authorities. He just laughed, said that wouldn't work, that he would kill them." She paused, blinking rapidly to clear the tears threatening to overflow.

She looked up at Dallas. "Do you really want to know what he said?" At his nod, she sighed. "I thought you would. He threatened to make me into a drug addict. If that didn't work, then he threatened to make me an alcoholic. He threatened to kidnap me and traffic me. If that didn't work, he threatened to kill me. He had all sorts of scenarios on how to do that, including taking me up in a friend's plane and shoving me out." She bit at her lip, drawing blood at how hard she did that. "Why would he do that?"

"Evil. Malice. Not getting what he wanted." Dallas looked down for a moment. "It wasn't you, actually, that he wanted, Ennis. He told you that but there are deeper reasons. One of them was revenge on Evan."

"Evan? Why?" Ennis was shocked, and she felt Bradon's arms tighten around her. She raised her head to stare at Dallas and then looked up at Bradon, seeing his love and compassion for her on his face. "I don't understand."

"I talked to Evan. I didn't tell him what I just told you. Apparently, Evan and his friends would make sure the young ladies were safe. He never told you that, I gather. His friends didn't tell him how bad it was for you because they knew he would go after Jason. They didn't want that. I gather they have told him some of it now. I've talked to them. Jason was all what you said and more. We are just so thankful God protected you. You have a lot of memories and feelings and whatnot to overcome, but you are doing just that. Bradon is helping you."

"I will continued to do that, Ennis, no matter what happens. I hope you understand that."

"I do, Bradon. But Dallas, there has to be more than what you're saying."

"There is, Ennis. A lot more." He stood, reaching for their cups. "I'm going to make myself to home, Ennis, and make fresh coffee. We're going to need that. What can I get you?" He walked away, leaving Ennis staring after him before she looked up at Bradon.

"Bradon?"

Bradon's arms tightened around his lady. "That's a lot to take in, Ennis. I thought it would be bad, but nothing like this. You should never have had to live with that."

"I know, but it happened. Now, what do we do? Where do we go with this?"

Chapter 44

Dallas stood for a moment, his eyes watching his friends, letting them talk quietly between themselves for a moment. Lord, this is just so hard. And how do we keep Evan from feeling as guilty as I know he will? He loves his sister deeply and would do just about anything, I suspect, to protect her.

Ennis watched Dallas as he walked back into the living room, accepting with a quiet word of thanks the cup of tea he handed her. Her eyes moved around the room, taking in the soft green of the walls, the light hardwood floors, the colourful rug, the dark brown of the furniture. She had set some of her knickknacks around, but it still didn't feel like home, she didn't think. She refused to look at Bradon, even thought she knew he was studying her.

Finally turning back to Dallas, she opened her mouth and then snapped it closed. She had no idea what she wanted to ask him, and she didn't think she could just come right out and ask who he suspected. She knew the Russells were involved somehow, just how, she wasn't sure.

"Dallas? What can you tell us?" Bradon finally broke the silence, his head tilting as he heard the door open, and then frowned as he saw his friends filing in. "Guys?"

Branigan shook his head. "We knew Dallas would be here. We wanted to sit in on what he has to say, if that's okay with you both." He watched as

Kade moved among the men, heading for Ennis, barely acknowledging Bradon. He's got a problem there, doesn't he, Lord? He has to reclaim his dog and I don't know that he will. Do I see another dog in the family?

"That's fine with me, Branigan." Ennis frowned at Dallas. "Okay, Dallas. Talk. Tell us where we stand."

There was a moment of shocked silence before the men laughed, knowing Ennis had done that on purpose to try and relieve the stress they were all under.

Dallas shook his head, a smile on his face. He caught the look on Bradon's face and sensed that Bradon knew what might be coming.

"Ennis? How well did you know Paul Baker?"

"Paul Baker? I don't think I know him. Should I."

Dallas nodded. "We have found evidence that he was also tracking you. Not for Jason. but for the Russells."

"Why?"

Brandon spoke up, "That is something we wanted to talk to you both about."

"I don't get it." Ennis frowned before her brow cleared and she nodded, "I can remember him. I just forgot or wanted to forget,". She sighed. "Another cousin, I think."

"That's correct, Ennis." Dallas opened the folder he had dropped to the table when he entered.

His eyes rested on the photo before he handed it to her. "Do you know who this is?"

Bradon watched as she took the photo, a frown on her face as she looked down and then froze.

"I know this man. I don't know his name. He was always in the background when Jason approached me. Who is he?" She looked up at Dallas, her face white and drawn. "Is he the one behind it all? He looks about our age."

"He is, Ennis." Dallas paused, biting his lip, uncertainly in his manner. He didn't know how to tell Ennis who this was.

"Dallas?" Bradon's voice caught at his attention, and he looked over at him, seeing the concern on his face. "Who is it?"

Ennis was shaking enough that the other men were concerned. She didn't know her parents and Anna were standing just inside the kitchen doorway, their eyes on the group scattered throughout the living room. Meg wanted to go to her daughter, but knew Ennis would not want that. Ian's face was drawn into grim lines. Branigan and Breck had approached him the night before with what they had found. He knew it likely matched what Dallas had, just by what he had said.

Finally raising her head, Ennis looked up at Bradon. "I'm sorry, Bradon. I'm so sorry. I didn't know. I didn't realize he was there all the time."

"Who?" Bradon waited before he asked again. "Who is it, Ennis?"

"A third cousin of mine. I never knew." She didn't hear the gasp from her mother as she turned to Ian, who nodded. "I wish I had. I never liked to be around him. I guess this is why." She studied the men, seeing their compassion and caring for her on their faces. "That's Jack Dixon."

Dallas nodded. "We have enough evidence to arrest him and will do just that. Ennis, it is imperative that you stay safe. You can't be out and about until we find him."

Ennis shook her head. "I can't stay locked away. I never could." She struggled to rise, kept in her place by Bradon's arms around her. "Bradon?"

"Just listen, sweetheart. That's all we ask. And if you are going to be out and about, one of the guys will be with us."

"You need to stay away from me. I just know he's the one who did this to you."

She heard the murmuring of agreement from the men and then leaned back on Bradon, her eyes on Dallas.

"I want this over with, Dallas. How much time do you need?"

Dallas looked up from his phone. "I just got word. He was found, Ennis, about an hour ago."

"Good. Then you can talk to him and this will be over for me." She didn't catch the look on Dallas' face.

"Ennis, sweetheart, I don't think it's over." Bradon could hear the mutters coming from his friends, who had picked up on what Dallas hadn't said yet.

"Bradon?" She looked up at him before her eyes swung back to Dallas. "Dallas? You found him? You've arrested him?" When he shook his head, her eyes slid closed. "He's dead, isn't he? Then, how do we find the ones responsible?"

"That is where we come in, Ennis. Bradon." Barnabas spoke, sharing a look with the other men. "We have done a lot of research and, Dallas, we have copies of it all for you. Some or I guess a lot of it has been verified by other police forces as they were investigating as well."

Dallas nodded. "That's great. We'll certainly take a look at it and add it to our investigations. Are you sure you're not detectives?"

The men laughed at him before sobering.

"We're not, Dallas, but we want this over for these two." Burnie spoke up. "If we find more, we will certainly pass it on to you."

Ennis watched the men closely, seeing the soberness they were trying hard to hide. This is it, isn't it, Lord? We are not there yet, as Evan would say. When will we be? I need to move on, to overcome what I've lived with for so many years. And when I can move on, so can Bradon. Just, dear Lord, keep him and his friends safe. Give us the peace and courage we need to face what's upcoming, and I know it's going to be big and going to hurt in so many ways.

Chapter 45

Two days later, Bradon stood by his truck door, a hand out to steady Ennis as she slid from the seat and then balanced the crutches under her arms. She had wanted to come to town, needed to, she told him. He had shaken his head and then helped her out to his truck.

Bradon raised his head, searching, feeling watched but not seeing who it was. He knew some of his friends would be there, he just wasn't sure who. His eyes dropped to Ennis, seeing the strain in her face, the fatigue, the pain caused not just by her physical injuries but by the emotional and mental, and yes, spiritual, pain that she had endured for so long.

"Where to?" His question brought Ennis' eyes to him.

"I'm not sure." She sighed, holding up one of her crutches. "I'm not walking too far, I suspect. Maybe, just maybe, this wasn't such a great idea."

"We'll make do. We'll look around here. Then, back in the truck you go, and we move down the street." He grinned at the frown she threw him.

Ennis sighed. "This is so hard, you know. And the doctor said he can't guarantee this will work. I still might face surgery because of them."

"If you do, we'll all be there for you. None of us are walking away from you." Bradon held the door open to a small diner, watching closely as she stood for a moment, lost in thought, before she shook her head and then looked up at him, a look in her eyes that gave him hope she returned his feelings.

Branigan studied the area around the diner, looking for someone who was out of place, but not seeing anyone. He could feel the prickles on the back of his neck, and knew someone was out there, but who and where? Brennen spoke form beside him.

"Someone is out here. But where?" He spun in a slow circle, his eyes narrowed as he searched.

"I know there is." Branigan nodded towards the diner. "We may as well go in and watch from there. Did you know that this was where he was heading?"

Brennen shrugged. "He asked her about going out for a meal. I'm not sure this is what she had in mind coming into town, but it gets her out. She's starting to wear thin."

"She is. She's had this over her head since she was, what fifteen or sixteen?"

"Something like that. Baird and I talked to Evan. He's devastated with what Dallas told him. He had no idea it was that bad or that his friends had picked up for him without telling him. They all think of Ennis as a younger sister."

"I thought it would be bad for him." Branigan slid into a chair at a table where he could watch the door and also Bradon and Ennis. "I never thought, when we hired on with Barnabas, that it would come to this."

———

"I don't think any of us did. For four of us to go through this, it makes you wonder if your own turn is next."

Branigan nodded as he accepted the menu, laying it down to the wooden table top, moving his utensils to one side to do so. "It does, but then, God is in control here, isn't He? He has let each of us to gain the knowledge we need to help one another." He looked around. "Someone is in here that's watching them."

"I know. I can feel them, but I can't see who."

Ennis looked up, catching Branigan's eye, and then looked across the booth at Bradon.

"Branigan and Brennen are here. Did you know they were following us?"

Bradon gave a grim smile even as he nodded. "I knew someone would. That's what they've told me they would do. Dallas has said if they don't, he has volunteers from the force to do just that."

"Volunteers? Like police officers?"

"Just like that. On their own time at that." He suddenly smiled, the smile lighting up his face. "So, here we are. On a date. What would you like?"

"A date is it?" It took Ennis a moment to shift her thoughts. "I don't know. I don't think this was that great an idea." She chewed at her lip even as her eyes dropped to the menu. "I don't know what I want. Just order something for me."

"Ennis?" Bradon's hand reached to still the hand she was rubbing on the table top. "If you don't want to eat, we'll leave. Find something else to do.

Go home. But you need to get out, restricted as it is for you."

She studied him and then beckoned for the waitress, a frown on Bradon's face as she did so.

"So, tell me, what is the best thing here on the menu to eat?"

The waitress smiled. "That would be the fish and chips. The best in town."

"Then, that's what we'll both have. He has coffee and what kind of teas do you have? An Irish one by chance?"

"We do." The waitress gathered their menus and headed away, leaving Bradon staring at Ennis, mouth open, as she smirked at him.

Later, they stopped beside Branigan and Brennen, who both watched closely around them.

"Brennen? I think we're heading back to the building. Ennis is tired enough she's almost asleep on me." Bradon watched her as she teased Branigan, a smile on her face that didn't quite reach her eyes.

"She is. Head out. We'll be right behind you." He looked around. "There is someone here, Bradon. Take all the precautions you can. Both Branigan and I felt the presence in the diner, but couldn't pick out just one person."

"And you won't. Whoever it is, that person is known to you. You won't suspect who it is." Ennis had caught Brennen's words.

Bradon headed for the road home, not thinking of the route he was driving, his thoughts instead on

———

Ennis. She is so special, Lord. She's the lady I've been looking for, but didn't know. Only thing is, she has so much to overcome. I don't want to rush her, but I don't want to lose her. He felt peace flow through his heart and almost the touch of a hand on his head. He knew God had heard and would honour his request, if that was His will for them both.

He slammed on the brakes suddenly, a car appearing across the road. He frantically looked around, shoving the truck into reverse, seeing Brennen doing the same before Brennen came to an abrupt halt. They were boxed in, with nowhere to go. He heard the soft cry from Ennis and turned, seeing a masked man appearing at her door, a weapon raised and pointed directly at her.

Chapter 46

Reaching for her hand, Bradon watched Ennis carefully before he heard the tap on his own window and sighed. This is it, isn't it, Lord? He slid from the truck, ignoring the motions to move away and walked around to help Ennis out and get balanced on her crutches.

Bradon stood, watching as Branigan and Brennen were shoved towards them, reluctance on their part. None of their assailants could be identified, masks covering their faces. His arm around her, he stood, waiting for what he wasn't sure. The men made no effort to force them away. It's almost as if they are waiting for someone to arrive, Bradon thought. He felt Ennis shift under his arm and looked down at her, seeing first a frown and then dawning understanding on her face.

"Ennis?" Bradon kept his voice low.

"That one behind Branigan? That's the Russell they've been looking at. I would suspect these are his sons and nephews. They all have similar builds and stances and looks on their faces." Ennis leaned into him, her leg aching, part from the stress she knew. "I just wonder when his boss will show up."

"You really expect that?" Bradon's hold tightened on her as his friends were forced over to stand beside him.

"Bradon?" Branigan's voice was low as well, barely audible. The noises from the surrounding trees and pond that had halted as the vehicles stopped, started up once more.

The men knew just how close they were to home. Brennen had managed to get off a text to Barnabas before he was forced from the truck. They just prayed Barnabas had received it and would appear to rescue them. At the moment, they held little hope out that that would happen.

Ennis frowned as she stared at the man she suspected was the eldest, the leader of the six men, and Bradon felt her move slightly.

"Ennis?"

"It's okay, Bradon. I know who this is. And I know who he'll be expecting." Ennis shifted to watch Branigan and Brennen, finding them watching the men in front of them. "There's no one behind us, is there?"

Bradon shook his head. "No, there isn't. But we can't get away that way. You can't run."

"I know that." Ennis was frustrated. "I just wanted to make sure they were all in front of us, with no one behind us. That's all. It makes it easier to watch them." She looked around. "What would you suggest?"

Branigan shook his head at her. "We can't do anything, Ennis. They have guns, in case you missed that."

"I know that. It's just we won't be surprised if someone walks up behind us." She looked around. "And I know that someone else is on the way here. They would have moved us away if not. What they are planning? For your friends to find our bodies here."

Brennen stared at her before he looked at the men. "I suspect that's their plan. Who would have thought of us being ambushed here."

"I would."

Bradon looked around. "What is here that they would want? Or need? Or desire to take us to?"

"There's the old cave, isn't there?" Brennen spoke up.

"No, not that. Is there a quarry, or a deep hole, or something like that?" Ennis was running scenarios through her mind, desperate to find some way to get the men away from her and to safety.

Branigan stared at her and then groaned. "There is. There's an old pit that is deep with steep sides. We wouldn't survive very well, if at all, if we were shoved down it."

"And that's their plan. Make us disappear. Take the trucks like to a scrap yard and trash them. No one would ever find us, now would they?" Ennis heard a faint rustle behind her and stiffened. Not that, Lord. Please, no one behind us. She looked up to see men rising up behind their captors, and shook her head slightly to halt their progress. She could feel the tension but relief in the way Bradon was holding her.

"Tim Russell! I know that's you. I know these are your sons and nephews. So stop hiding." Ennis's voice ringing out in accusation startled them at first. "Why did you do it?"

Tim Russell stepped forward, the mask dropping from his face. "Because of you. You stood in our way."

"And just how did I do that?" Ennis' anger showed in the way she spat out her words. "I didn't know you. I had nothing to do with you, or your sons. In fact, I ran as far from them as I could. So did all my friends and anyone else we warned." She paused, a sudden thought drawing a deep breath from her.

"And I would say that is it, Ennis." Bradon's arm tightened on her as he heard low mutters from his two friends. "You prevented something and didn't even realize it."

"And you did. You don't know how many times the ones we were after disappeared from our grasp or were only seen in a group. It was because of you. You wrecked a network we had set up." Tim's anger at Ennis had his body shaking, and the loudness of his voice stilled the sounds around them once more. "You have to pay."

Ennis shook her head. "I don't think so. Not this time. You've taken enough from me. Years I should have enjoyed as a teenager and a young lady. That, I can never get back. God have mercy on your souls, Tim, because I sure don't. You have ruined how many lives? Look at your own family? Your sons are following in your footsteps. Did they really want that? What about your daughters? I've seen them around town. They are beaten down, unhappy, and afraid. You've done that to them.

"And how many people have you done that to in your line of work? Is that why witnesses to crimes disappear and aren't seen again? You threaten them. I would even say at times you've stooped to murder. How close am I?"

Ennis was taunting him, hoping to break his silence. She knew one of Bradon's friends was recording it. She wasn't sure who from the camouflage they had on, but he had waved his phone at her.

Tim spun, his eyes on the men with him, not seeing the men standing back from him, or seeing the police officers moving in behind them. He spun back to face her, charging at her, to miss her as Bradon pulled her to one side, her crutches clattering to the ground as she dropped them. Tim lost his balance, falling heavily to the ground, where he lay, the breath knocked out of him. He didn't hear the words for his family to drop their weapons, or their rights being read to them. He felt his hands pulled behind him and cuffs around his wrists before he was pulled to his feet.

Dallas watched the activity closely before he approached the four, his head tiling to study Ennis even as Brennen handed her the crutches she had dropped.

"Ennis?"

"Dallas? Is it over?" Ennis had hope in her heart but doubted that it was

"It is. We stopped and arrested the mayor's assistant. Brady sent us a text as to what was going on and kept us updated as we arrived. It was a brave thing you did.”

Ennis shrugged. “It had to be done. God chose me to do it. I just wish He hadn’t. I wish this had never happened.” She clumped away from them on her crutches, heading for the building she knew was up ahead. Bradon watched, not moving to follow her, surprise on his friends’ faces.

“Bradon? Aren’t you going after her?”

Bradon shook his head. “I can’t. I have to let her have time to absorb this, to heal. If I don’t, at some point, she’ll resent me and walk away for good.” He turned and walked from them, heading for his truck, where he slid behind the wheel and just sat, his eyes watching Ennis as she struggled to walk, until Burnie approached her and stopped her, then led her to a vehicle.

Is this it, Lord? Does she walk away for good? Or will she be back? I hope You know she’s taking my heart with her. There will never be another one for me. But I need to let her have this time. Protect and heal her, please, Dear Lord?

Chapter 47

A month later, Bradon sat on a rock near the lakeshore, watching the waves crashing up. It was a windy, damp day and he knew better than to just sit but he had no desire to do anything. He had been back to work and back to his volunteer duties, but his heart wasn't in it.

He felt the nudge of Kade's nose and absentmindedly rubbed at the dog's head, knowing how Kade felt. He felt the same.

"You miss her, don't you, boy? I know. So do I. I pray she comes back, but I don't think she will. It's just you and me again, fellow." He heard the deep sigh Kade gave, almost as if he understood his words.

Kade wandered the lakeshore, not even barking at the seagulls that tormented him. His head turned suddenly as he caught a familiar scent and he was away across the sand and the rocks, heading for a person he now saw walking towards them.

Bradon had missed Kade's flight, his thoughts deep and dark. He jumped as he felt a hand on his shoulder, not expecting anyone to be there. He rose, wonder in his eyes and on his face, as he stared down at Ennis.

"Ennis? You're here?"

"Bradon? Forgive me for walking away. It was just too much." Ennis stood, eyes raised to him, hope on her face, but hesitation and the fear that he would reject her in her bearing.

Bradon simply shook his head, swept her into his arms, and held her tightly, his tears wetting her hair, feeling her tears on his shirt and felt her arms around him. They stood, Kade watching, head tilting before he gave a bark. As far as he was concerned, his lady was back and with his master. That made life good for him. He finally laid down, nose on his paws, eyes raised to his people.

Ennis finally shoved back a bit, her eyes on Bradon, seeing the emotions roiling on his face, but uppermost, she saw his love for her. *I didn't lose it after all, did I, Lord? Thank you.*

"Ennis? You're okay?" He pulled her down to the rock he had been sitting on, an arm tight around her, her head on his shoulder.

"I'm getting there. I had to leave you that day, Bradon. I was a broken mess of humanity. I have been in counselling with a friend, had it out with Mom and Dad and Evan, found some friends I thought I had lost. Buckley has kept in touch."

"He has? That doesn't surprise me. That's who he is." He paused, just content to hold his love. "Has Dallas spoken to you?"

"He has. We've met a number of times, in fact. He told me Tim Russell hasn't confessed, so he'll be going to trial. His sons and nephews have, and they're facing what they need to." She paused. "Did you suspect the assistant at all?"

Bradon shook his head. "Not one bit. Did you?"

She nodded. "I did. I know her. She's always been a bit shady, as they say. She's not saying a word, Dallas tells me, but the wealth on information and evidence means she'll be facing a long prison term. It makes me sick to think of the lives they've ruined, the people lost to their families forever."

"It is a sick world, sweetheart. But we have God and that makes it bearable for us. All we can do is pray for them."

"That's all we can do. It was a struggle for me to get to that point, but I have found forgiveness for them. If I couldn't, then they would have won. I would never have overcome the obstacles I faced all my life."

"Those obstacles have made you who you are. The lady I love dearly and would like to spend the rest of my life with. Besides, Kade is moping. We can't have that." He smirked at her before he added. "Besides you asked and I said yes."

Ennis stared at him, her mouth open for a moment, before she laughed and then hugged him. "I did do that, didn't I? You know that's what you'll face. Me asking something as I drop off to sleep."

"I know, sweetheart, I know. I will delight in those very requests." He drew her to her feet, and taking her hand, led her back towards the building. "We need to make some plans. First, I talked to your Dad weeks ago. He didn't say anything, just looked thoughtful, and told me I had to take it up with you."

"He did? I guess he knew what had happened." She shook a finger at him as he laughed. "So, when will we set a wedding date?"

"Soon, I hope, sweetheart. We've lost time to those men."

"We did, dearest, but God was there. He knew what He was allowing. We needed to face my past before we could move to our present and our tomorrow."

"And just so you are aware, when we marry, the Foundation provides a salary for you." He watched her eyes grow round and a stunned look cross her face.

"They do that?"

Bradon nodded. "They do. They think a wife is valuable not only to her husband, but to God's work. By paying a salary, she can devote herself to her family and what she chooses to do. You don't have to work. You could volunteer. The choice is yours. And if you do decide to work, you are hired by a company at no charge to them."

Ennis shook her head, stunned at the revelation, and then a beautiful smile crossed her face. "God is so good to us, isn't He? He had this planned for us, all along."

"That He did, my love. That He did."

Two weeks later, Ennis stood, her hand tucked into her father's elbow, a sheet of peach roses in her hands, her eyes fastened on the door ahead of her. Bradon and she had decided they didn't want to wait long, that too much time had already been lost to them.

Ian watched his daughter closely, thankful beyond words that she was finally safe. He could see the changes in her, changes that her trials had wrought, but that had brought her to who she was. Lord, bless this couple. You planned this. You brought Bradon here from Alberta all those years ago. Your plans have come to fruition for these two. We welcome Bradon as another son.

Bradon turned later that afternoon, searching for Ennis, seeing her talking with Berneen, Cadee and Devaney. He was glad these four were friends. They would be a source of comfort and strength and joy for each other. He turned his head as he heard footsteps stop beside him.

"Bradon? You're okay?" Barnabas' voice was low. He was one who always checked to ensure his friends were healthy, happy and safe. With him, it went beyond mere employer and employee.

"I am, Barnabas. Thanks for asking. You're okay taking Kade for me?"

Barnabas laughed. "I am, but I don't think Kade is all that impressed. He thinks he needs to go with his lady."

Bradon joined him in laughter. "She is that. I don't know how we're going to work this, but we will. Kade has been like that all along with Ennis."

"He knew she was in danger. He also knew somehow that she would be important to you."

"That he did." Bradon reached to wrap Ennis in his arms, a quick kiss dropped on her mouth. He didn't hear Barnabas walk away.

Ennis had watched him. "Bradon, what's Barnabas' story?"

"His story? I'm sorry, I'm not sure what you mean."

"Has he never had a lady in his life?"

"Not that we've ever seen. And he keeps that close to himself. I sometimes wonder if there had been and he was hurt."

Bardon turned her to face the lake, watching the sun as it set, sending out the beautiful coloured rays it always did on days like this.

"I love you deeply, Ennis. Never doubt that."

She looked up at him, eyes shining with love and happiness. "I know, and I love you deeply as well. I know we'll have our struggles, our differences, sickness, whatever God allows. But He has already overcome those for us, hasn't He?"

Bradon continued to stare at the sky, his thoughts sifting through her words. He finally stared down at her upturned face. "You have said it so well. He is truly in everything with us, and has already given us the victory over it. We just need to trust Him."

Dear Readers

Thank you for picking up the story of Bradon and Ennis. Once more, I had no idea where they were heading or the ride they would take me, as the author, and you, as the readers, on as they never tell me until the words are actually appearing in the manuscript.

What do you have to overcome today? I pray that you will just place your hand in God's and know that He desires only the best for you. Sometimes He lets us go through struggles of many kinds in order to be refined to the person He desires us to be.

During the writing of this, we were still dealing with the COVID-19 lockdown. It has been tough but necessary. Once more, I can say, God has been in control, even though it seems He isn't. He could have stopped it, could have changed it, could have not allowed it in the first place. But He did. That's where trust and faith come in.

God bless each one of you.

Ronna